Madame Squidley and Beanie

Also by ALICE MEAD

Junebug
Adem's Cross
Junebug and the Reverend
Soldier Mom
Girl of Kosovo
Junebug in Trouble
Year of No Rain

Madame Squidley and Beanie

Alice Mead

FARRAR, STRAUS AND GIROUX • NEW YORK

www.fsgkidsbooks.com

Library of Congress Cataloging-in-Publication Data
Mead, Alice.
    Madame Squidley and Beanie / by Alice Mead.— 1st ed.
        p.   cm.
    Summary: Ten-year-old Beanie struggles with the start of a new school year,
being excluded from the fifth grade in-crowd, and the extra burdens her
mother's Chronic Fatigue Syndrome places on her.
    ISBN 0-374-34688-7
    [1. Chronic fatigue syndrome—Fiction.   2. Sick—Fiction.   3. Schools—
Fiction.   4. Friendship—Fiction.   5. Popularity—Fiction.]   I. Title.

PZ7.M47887Mad 2004
[Fic]—dc21

                                                            2003048057

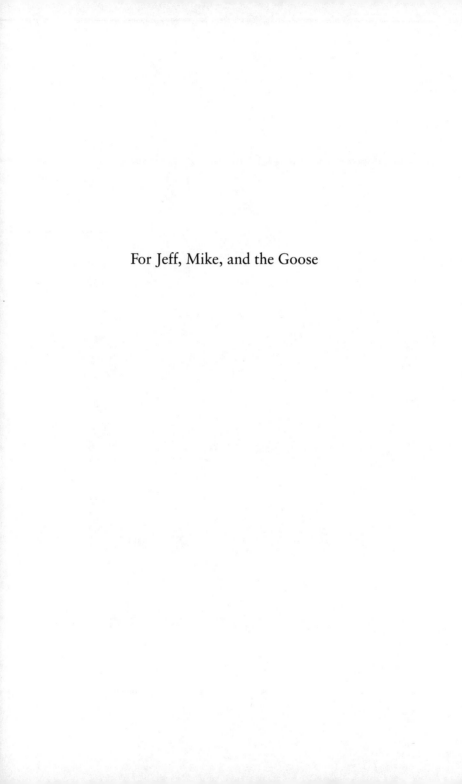

For Jeff, Mike, and the Goose

MADAME SQUIDLEY AND BEANIE

1

"Okay, guys. Have a good time," Nora Kingsley said. "And remember, I'll be at the doctor's, so Charles's mom will pick you up right here by the entrance at four. If I'm running much later than I expect, I'll call the house around four-thirty."

"Yeah, Mom, we know," Jerm said. Jerm was six, and his real name was Jeremiah Kingsley.

He and Charles Sprague were already climbing out of the car. Like Beanie, Charles was ten, and he lived directly across the street from the Kingsleys in the small town of Weymouth, Maine. His hair was blond and spiky and his face round, and he often wore an old Boy Scout shirt with the badges cut off, leaving darker-colored circles where they had been.

Beanie—really Beatrice—Kingsley slid across the seat and paused. Beanie had long, medium-brown hair and brown eyes. She wore faded gym shorts and an old Weymouth Day Camp polo shirt.

"We can remember that, Mom. It's no big deal."

But the problem was that for her mother now, it *was* a big deal. Remembering schedules, buying groceries, cooking—everything was. Her mom hadn't been back to work since last April, when she and Beanie had gotten sick with a bad case of the flu. Beanie had recovered, but her mother simply hadn't.

Since her illness, her mom couldn't remember schedules at all. She had been reading those times—"four o'clock, pick up kids; four-thirty, call home"—from a piece of notepaper that lay propped beside her on the seat. A bright yellow Post-It note was stuck to the dashboard with her doctor's name on it: Dr. Leo Howell, rheumatologist. 105 Sewell Street.

Feeling fretful and torn, Beanie sat half in and half out of the car. Part of her couldn't wait to pass through the festival gates; part of her wanted to stay with her mom and make sure everything went well at the appointment.

"How come your doctor can't give you some medicine to make you better?" she asked. It was the same question Beanie had asked on her mother's two previous trips to Dr. Howell.

"He has to confirm what's wrong. And he has to rule out some more serious problems," her mother answered. "You can't take medicine if you don't know exactly what you're taking it for."

"Serious problems? Like what? What could be more serious?" Beanie tugged at a strand of hair anxiously. She was by nature a worrywart.

"Nevermind that now, sweetie. Look: Jerm and Charles are waiting."

"Yeah," Beanie muttered. "I know."

Through the chain-link fence that surrounded the fairgrounds, she could see the tents and activities of Weymouth's annual August Lobster Festival. She could hear the screams of excited kids, smell the scent of popcorn and sawdust, and see colored lights swaying on cables strung between the exhibits, lit up and waiting for night, still many hours away.

"Beanie, come on!" Jerm said impatiently.

"Yeah, what's the delay, Beanbag?" Charles added.

What if Dr. Howell had bad news? What if her mom had a brain tumor or that illness old people got, Alzheimer's? Those were serious. Mrs. Kingsley was barely able to take care of Beanie and Jerm as it was.

"Should I go with you?" Beanie asked.

"No, no. This visit is just to get some lab results. It's nothing. You go on and have fun. Come on. Out you go!"

Beanie sighed. "Okay. Bye."

She climbed out of the car and slammed the door, then watched her mom pull onto the road.

"Beanie! Come on!" Jerm urged again. "Move it, girl!"

His sweatpants were torn at the knee, and the seat bagged out. His little round eyeglasses flashed sunlight at her. He wore a faded, much-too-small black T-shirt that said VISIT MAINE. She stuck out her tongue at him.

Why did she have to go to the festival with a scrawny six-year-old instead of a crowd of girls from her grade? She knew that none of the other girls who were sure to be here would be taking care of younger brothers and sisters. Beanie was worried about her mom, true, but that wasn't the whole story.

As she hurried after Charles and Jerm, she felt a sharp stab of self-pity and resentment that her mother wasn't strong or active anymore. Her mom always used to take them to the festival. Last year she had entertained Jerm on the kiddie rides while Beanie and Charles ran around with a group of their school friends. Her mother used to do a lot of things . . . But Beanie wouldn't think about that now. She was here to have fun.

Beanie stumbled after the boys through the dry weeds. On their street, Poplar Lane, there was a girl Beanie's age, named Miranda Adams. For the hundredth time at least, Beanie wished that Mrs. Adams, Miranda's mom, were her mother. And she wished that Miranda, one of the popular girls in school, were her best friend.

⁓

They quickly bought their tickets. Today, August 30, 2000, was half-price day for kids under fifteen, and the festival was mobbed with kids dashing around in excitement.

"Let's do the Haunted House first," Jerm called out. "This way, you guys."

He started to rush ahead through the crowd, but Charles seized his arm.

"Wait, Jerm," Charles said. "We don't want to get separated in the first five minutes."

"He never waits," Beanie said. "You are so lucky you're an only child."

"Yeah? I don't think so," Charles said. "My parents worry about me too much. Have you ever seen them out in the driveway, fighting about my back brace? My mom wants me to wear it. My dad thinks I shouldn't. Blah, blah, blah. I have to put it on as soon as we get home."

"I know they don't agree about it," Beanie replied, "but I hadn't noticed the fighting."

"Yeah, well, keep an eye out. Things have reached a fever pitch."

Charles had scoliosis. His parents were divorced, and his dad lived a half hour away. Beanie and Jerm's dad was dead. He'd died when Jerm was a baby and Beanie was four. Their only other relatives were their Uncle Ozzy and Auntie Jane in San Francisco. Beanie and Jerm saw them once a year at Christmas.

"What do you do when they fight?" Beanie asked.

"I sit in the car and hold my breath, seeing if I can turn blue."

Beanie laughed. "No you don't."

"Yes I do. I want to act as weird as they do."

"Your mom is kind of whacked."

"Kind of? Ha!"

"She's nice, though. Hey!" Beanie cried suddenly. "Look. A fortune-teller's tent. Wait for me, you guys, while I go in."

"Beanie, don't. It's a rip-off," Charles said. "Save your tickets for the Cobra and the Octopus."

"Just wait for me."

"Oh, man," wailed Jerm. "This is going to take forever." He flopped down on the grass.

"Goodbye, Charles. Adiós, Jerm." Beanie saluted them. "I'm going in."

Charles cupped his hands to his mouth and announced in a deep voice, "She's going in, folks. She's going in."

Beanie grinned. Then she approached the purple tent cautiously, tickets clutched in her hand.

2

THE SIGN OUT FRONT READ: FORTUNES BY MADAME Olivia. Beanie hoped Madame Olivia would tell her that her mother's doctor's appointment would go well that afternoon, that there was absolutely nothing to be worried about, and that her mother would make a full recovery. As Beanie parted the flaps and entered, the spicy-sweet smell of burning incense greeted her. It made the inside of her nose tickle.

"Tickets, please." Madame Olivia wore a gold turban and had enormous blood-red fingernails (fake ones, thought Beanie knowingly) and long black curls (a wig?). She gestured for Beanie to sit on an old-fashioned wooden stool with claw feet. The small square table that held the crystal ball was draped with a gold brocade cloth, and fat candles in bronze holders flickered in each corner of the tent, casting the folds and crags of Madame Olivia's face into deep shadow.

"Well? Give me your right hand," Madame Olivia said.

Obediently, Beanie thrust out her hand, palm up. Madame Olivia inspected it carefully. Beanie hoped she wouldn't say anything about her nails, which Beanie had been biting earlier that day. And she very much hoped that Madame Olivia wouldn't say anything about how often Beanie pulled on the end of her nose because it was too short. Barbie Leighton, Miranda's friend and leader of the Snob Squad, said Beanie's nose looked piggy.

Beanie shifted her gaze while she waited with her arm stretched out. In the center of the table sat the shiny crystal ball. "Madame Olivia, is, um, anything secret about me going to appear in that ball?" Beanie asked.

"Silence."

"Sorry," Beanie said. She looked at the candles instead, and tried not to think about her mom slipping on the stairs last week, or dropping the salad bowl, so that little slices of carrot rolled across the floor like orange-colored wheels, or stumbling over the edge of the carpet while she was carrying a load of laundry.

What if Beanie's most absolutely secret wish did appear in the shiny ball? She would see her ideal dream family, the perfect, beautiful, rich Adamses, drive up to her school in a stretch limousine to take her away from her messed-up family with the sick mom, the dad killed in a car crash long ago, and the little brother who thought he was a genius but was really just a big buttinsky. Did Madame Olivia have the power to see that? Beanie wasn't quite sure.

"I suppose you want to hear about your future," Madame Olivia said finally with a heavy sigh. "Right?

The four healthy children, winning the lottery, and all that?"

"Maybe you could just tell me my present. You see, I think . . . Well, it sounds kind of silly, but it might be possible that there was a mix-up in the hospital when I was born, and I went home with the wrong family. I have proof. They have these great big noses, you see, and I have this short, stubby one—"

Madame Olivia held up her hands to silence Beanie. "Stop. Please. How can I hear the voices from the Great Beyond with all this childish chatter going on?"

"But can I just say one more thing? My mom is sick, and she really can't take care of us very well. Well, she thinks she can, but she hasn't been able to work since April. She might have to quit her job altogether, and then we'll be poor and—"

"Hush!" Frowning, Madame Olivia dropped Beanie's palm abruptly. She crossed her legs, pulled an emery board from the bodice of her puffy-sleeved blouse, and started to file her fake-looking nails. "You want to hear about the present? That's absurd. You already know what's going on. You just told me your mother is ill." She blew away the invisible nail-file dust.

"But what if there was this terrible mistake? I mean, what if my real family is actually very wealthy? What if they have a limousine? And they are very healthy. They never ever get sick, not even with the flu. And they have medium-sized noses . . ."

Madame Olivia pursed her lips and stared at Beanie. "Are you quite finished?" she asked.

Beanie nodded.

"You want to trade in the family you've got? Sort of a self-pitying little wretch, aren't you?"

"No. I mean, maybe."

"You want to be driven about in a limousine? There is absolutely no limousine in your future. You can forget about that!"

Madame Olivia put on a pair of reading glasses and bent over the crystal ball, shifting her gaze from side to side as though to get a better look. "Hmmmm. Something's wrong, that's obvious. Your future is clouded. Like a bank of fog. Very, very sorrowful and damp fog. But! What's this? You will take a voyage of discovery near a mountain," Madame Olivia said. "That's all I can tell you."

Beanie gasped. "A voyage? With my mom and little brother? Or all by myself?"

"By yourself."

"Please, can you look again?"

"Heavens, no, I can't look again. I said a voyage near a mountain. I believe the fog is mist rising off a lake."

"A lake and a mountain voyage? If I went on a voyage by myself, wouldn't it be like running away from home? I'm only ten. Or—oh! Do you mean maybe my mom is . . . I mean, she's not going to . . ."

"What's wrong with a voyage? I thought you just said you wanted to leave your family. Anyway, do you think the universe cares what age you are or even what you want? That's all. Please go. All this jibber-jabber is wearing me out. Be thankful you have a mother, for heaven's sake."

Beanie stood up. "Thank you," she said in a small voice.

"My pleasure," Madame Olivia said, rolling her eyes.

Beanie turned and opened the door flap. A sorrowful fog? A voyage all by herself? Beanie pushed her way out of the tent.

"What happened? What did she say?" Charles asked impatiently.

"You were in there forever," Jerm added.

"Not forever. Eight minutes," Charles said, glancing at his big, black, scientific-looking watch.

"It was jumbled up. It was stupid. She didn't really tell me anything," Beanie replied, thinking of how the fortune-teller had said she was ungrateful and self-pitying.

"But she must have said something in all that time," Charles insisted.

"She didn't tell me anything that I didn't know, that's all. Come on. I'll race you to the Teacups." The twirling Teacups ride was a traditional rendezvous spot for fifth- and sixth-grade girls.

"The Teacups? Hey, I thought we were going to the Haunted House. Beanie! Wait up!" Jerm hollered.

3

BUT ALREADY BEANIE WAS RUNNING THROUGH THE crowd, dodging baby strollers and big, round beer bellies, sticky spires of pink or blue cotton candy and buckets of oily yellow popcorn, sullen teenagers in heavy metal T-shirts, and little kids with large cups of sweet Orange Crush.

The twirling Teacups was one of the busiest rides, and the long line that doubled back on itself meant at least a fifteen-minute wait. They joined the line at the end.

Suddenly Beanie clutched Charles's arm. "Oh, no! Charles, look! There's Ernestine Brown. I hope she doesn't head this way."

"Isn't she in 4-H club? I think she raises sheep," Charles said. "Yep. Check it out. She's covered with bits of straw."

"Let's get out of here. Come on!" Beanie whispered urgently. "Before she sees us."

"I'm going to say hi," Jerm said teasingly.

"No you're not!" Beanie grabbed his hand and pulled him. "Come on."

"Hi, Ernestine!" Jerm hollered over his shoulder. "Yoo-hoo."

Ernestine, wearing overall cutoffs, her bushy auburn hair flying out around her face, turned her head, trying to see who had called her.

"Jerm," hissed Beanie. "Shut up!"

"Yeah, Jerm. Beanie's right. Ernestine is one of the world's most annoying people. She can ruin just about anything she puts her mind to."

But they'd already been spotted.

"Hey!" hollered Ernestine, bearing down on them. "Wait up."

"Hi," Beanie said lamely.

"Guess what? I'm in the sheep finals," Ernestine said, pulling a long yellow piece of straw out of her hair. "You should come see me."

"You're a sheep?" Charles asked with apparent innocence.

"No, peanut head. My sheep, Marissa, is in the finals. I just shampooed her and gave her a fluffing and a blow-dry."

"You shampooed a sheep?" Jerm said.

"Is this your little brother?" Ernestine asked.

"Yes," Beanie answered. "But we're not going on the Teacup ride now. The line's too long. Come on, guys. See you, Ernestine."

"You're baby-sitting? Too bad. The Snob Squad is here—Barbie, Miranda, and company. So listen, my sheep will be in the 4-H ring at five. You guys better be there to cheer me on."

"We can't. We're leaving at four," Charles said.

"Four?" shrieked Ernestine. "What a bunch of babies. Big fat babies, wearing big fat diapers. Where are you going now?"

"To the Haunted House. But don't come with us. You're really rude," Jerm said. "You know that?"

Ernestine burst out laughing, and as they hurried off, she continued to laugh, holding her stomach and staggering along behind them.

"That whole scene was your fault, Jerm," Beanie said angrily. "Now she's going to follow us."

"What did I do?"

"You called her over."

"We might have stumbled into her on our own," Charles said, trying to be Mr. Reasonable.

"Hey! Hey! Wait up!" Here came Ernestine, charging after them. "I'll do the Haunted House with you. My mom is watching Marissa for me to make sure she doesn't get dirty. I am not, I repeat not, washing her again!"

If they bumped into Miranda Adams and Barbie Leighton now, Beanie was sure she would die.

"Ernestine in the Haunted House. This should be an experience," whispered Charles.

"Yeah. No kidding."

The Haunted House was an old tractor-trailer parked in a far corner of the fairgrounds. Loudspeakers on its roof blared screams and groans and the sound of clanking chains. The carnival person in charge of admission was wearing a witch hat and green makeup and was reading last week's newspaper.

The four kids handed over their tickets. Pushing and shoving one another in excitement, they hurried up the ramp to the sound of a loudly creaking door and a deep-bass butler type of voice saying, "Do come in," followed by an evil, cackling laugh. They rushed inside.

In the first room, the floor was sharply tilted, and uneven black-and-white lines were drawn on the walls. Instantly, Beanie felt very dizzy.

"This floor is really flat, you know," Charles said. "I saw a program about optical illusions on TV and they showed how this floor is straight but those black-and-white lines—"

"Charles! Shut up. Obviously it's tilted. Look. We can't stand up," Ernestine said. "Just because something was on TV doesn't make it true."

"I'm going to barf," Jerm said. "Beanie? I think I—"

"Oh no you're not," Beanie said quickly. "Come on."

The kids staggered and zigzagged their way unsteadily across the tilting room to the door at the far end, which seemed to be at the top of a steep hill. They entered a long corridor where now the floor was made of spinning circles that looked like large tiddlywinks. As they spun, the kids had to jump from one tiddlywink to another the whole length of the corridor.

"This is easy. This is so, so easy," Jerm kept yelling out.

But when they reached the end of the tiddlywinks, without warning the lights went out. The children were engulfed in total darkness. The deep voice gave a long, eerie laugh. They heard clanking chains, then groans.

"Do you think the power went off?" Beanie said.

"No, or we wouldn't hear those creaks and groans and stuff. Don't worry. There'll be an exit sign," Charles said. "By law there has to be an exit sign."

Now Ernestine began to cackle. Beanie wrapped her arms around herself so she wouldn't accidentally bump into Ernestine. She looked this way and that, trying to see Charles or Jerm or perhaps an exit sign in the blackness.

But there was no sign.

"Oh, wow. So what? Pitch-dark. What's the big deal?" Beanie heard Jerm's squeaky voice pierce the utter blackness from off to her right. "I'm not scared one bit!"

"Grrrrarf!" shrieked Ernestine. "Tickle, tickle, eat a pickle."

"Ahhhh!" Jerm cried. "Let go of me!"

"Ha, ha. Gotcha!" Ernestine laughed.

"Hey! I found a doorway. Come on," Charles said, but he sounded far away.

"I'm here!" Beanie answered, putting her arms out in front of her, trying to feel her way through the dark. "I'm over here. Jerm? Charles?"

She heard their feet thudding rapidly, moving away from her. No one answered. Carefully she inched forward, sliding her sneakers along the floor in case there was a drop-off.

"Jerm?" she said again. "Hey, guys, where are you? You're not being funny. Say something."

She waited, but heard nothing. The darkness covered her face like a black cloth. Suddenly, ooof. She stubbed her toe. Ouch. Her outstretched hands banged against a door frame. That was a relief. A way out.

But now there was a ramp downward, steep. She inched along, then plunged forward, frightened. *Thump, thump, thump.* Her feet pounded down the ramp much faster than she meant to go.

A strobe light flashed, almost blinding her. Right afterward she saw a woman hunched in a wheelchair, with a deformed, terrible face. A laugh, another flash. A man, dead, rose from a casket.

Beanie screamed and covered her face with her hands. When she took them away again, she saw that the lights had come on. A curtain covered the entire gruesome scene. She ran into the next room.

There was Charles in his beat-up green hiking shorts and Ernestine dancing a jig and Jerm in his sweatpants torn at the knee, standing in front of a row of mirrors that made them fat and short or stretched out and thin. All three were making weird faces and laughing.

"I am so mad at you!" Beanie yelled at them. "Didn't you hear me calling?"

"This place is cool," Jerm said. "Look. Check out my face. Watch."

Ernestine grabbed Beanie's arm and dragged her in front of the mirror that made everyone look bulgy and fat. Horrible! Beanie was not in the mood.

"Let go of me, Ernestine. This is not cool at all. Let's get out of here."

"Beanie, what are you talking about?" Charles asked. "What's wrong?"

"I hate being scared like that, today especially. You guys don't even care. Mom's at the doctor right now. And maybe she has some terrible thing wrong with her. And you don't care."

Jerm and Charles looked at each other. Ernestine stared at Beanie.

"I want to leave. Now. I mean it, you guys."

"Wow, Beanie," Ernestine said. "You are really freaking out."

"Okay, okay," said Charles mildly. "Come on, Jerm. Let's try to stay together for a change."

They entered a mad scientist's basement laboratory, went through a mousehole into a room filled with giant stuffed mice and huge pieces of cheese, then crossed a torture chamber and a bat-filled attic, and stumbled out through a slowly spinning barrel. It was over. They were back outside, standing next to the tractor-trailer with electric cables as thick as snakes running every which way through the trampled grass at their feet.

"I hated that place," Beanie said. "It was horrible."

"It was awesome," Jerm said. "Now let's go get some cotton candy. We can eat it on line at the Teacups."

"Sure, Jerm," Beanie said, relieved that no one had teased her about being scared.

"Yeah, we can rot our teeth," Charles said. "And get fat." He wanted to become a doctor.

"And dye our tongues blue," said Ernestine.

"And get ugly pimples," Jerm said.

"And have heart attacks," Charles said.

"Good. My dad is a cardiologist," Ernestine said.

"Okay! Okay!" Beanie shouted. "Jeez."

"Jeez yourself. You're such a pain, Beanie," Jerm said.

"My nerves are on edge," Beanie said.

"Would you guys cut it out?" Charles said. "Could you all just shut up? Come on."

He headed for the cotton candy booth. Jerm chattered to Charles and Ernestine the whole way, but Beanie paid no attention. Then they got on line, waiting for the paper conefuls of warm, spun blue sugar.

"Hey, Beanie," Jerm said. "Look. There's Miranda and her creepy friend."

"Oh! Hi!" Beanie said, embarrassed to see Miranda standing at the head of the cotton candy line with Barbie Leighton. Now the girls would see she'd had to come to the fair with Jerm, and worse yet, they would think that she and Charles were best friends with Ernestine. Beanie's heart sank.

"Hi, Beanie. Hi, Charles. Hi, Ernestine. Ready for

school yet?" Miranda asked. "We went shopping for clothes today."

"Actually, I—" Beanie began, then stopped.

That was another thing that was hard for her mom now. Shopping. Especially at the mall. It was way too much walking. Beanie wasn't sure she was going back-to-school shopping for anything they couldn't get at the grocery store.

Of course, Mrs. Adams would have taken the girls. She could probably spend hours and hours at the mall. She played tennis at a fitness club and looked youthful and strong. She had even won a tournament.

"Come on, Miranda," said Barbie.

"Where are you guys going now?" Beanie called, desperately wanting to join them. She stared after the two girls wistfully.

"We'll be at the Teacups," Miranda called back. Over her shoulder, she shouted, "We're meeting some kids there! See ya!"

Ernestine glanced at her watch. "Uh-oh. I have to go, too. Don't forget. Five o'clock at the 4-H ring."

"We're going home at four," Jerm said. "Remember?"

"Oh, yeah. Well, see ya," Ernestine replied.

"Bye," Beanie mumbled as Ernestine galloped off through the crowd.

"Hey. Here you go, Beanbag. Take it," Charles said. "Cotton candy, dude. So good for you. One hundred percent sugar, chockablock full of blue dye. Yum."

"Thanks," Beanie muttered, biting into the sugary confection. "I wish we could go with those guys."

"Why are you always trying to be friends with Miranda, anyway? She's such a snob."

"She's so perfect, you mean." Beanie stared at the two girls in the distance. "Nothing bad has ever, ever happened to her. And her mother is wonderful, don't you think?"

"I like your mom much better. And Miranda perfect? Perfectly spoiled, maybe," Charles said. "Come on, Bean Brain. We're here to have fun and do crazy stuff. Forget those guys."

4

AT FOUR, MRS. SPRAGUE MET THEM AT THE CARNI-val entrance and drove them home.

The kids were quiet in the car. Beanie was relieved to get away from the noise and crowds. She had hated the clamor of the festival this year, and found herself longing for the cool woods of her own backyard. For the past two years on Labor Day weekend, Beanie's family had gone camping at Loon Lake. It was so calm and quiet there, and the air smelled fresh and piney-sweet. But would they go this year? Her mom hadn't said a word about it. Beanie would miss it.

"What's up?" Charles asked Beanie.

"Oh, nothing. Just tired, I guess."

"You guys want to play four square later?" he asked.

"Charles," Mrs. Sprague said, "you have to put your brace on, you know."

"Yeah, yeah." He looked at Beanie with his eyes crossed.

She laughed. Then they all rode in silence to Poplar Lane.

"Thanks for the ride, Mrs. Sprague," Beanie said. Charles's mom was a drama and film professor at the university in Portland. She had wild, dyed blond hair. "See you later, Charles. Come on, Jerm."

Jerm and Beanie raced each other to the back door.

"Hey, guys. How was the carnival?" Mrs. Kingsley asked as they tromped through the kitchen and flopped into chairs in the living room.

Beanie's mom had curly dark hair, a sprinkle of pale freckles, and a wide, smiling mouth.

"It was great!" said Jerm.

"Okay, I guess," answered Beanie.

"What was great?" her mother asked.

"The Haunted House!" Jerm burst in. "I'm going to make one in the basement and charge everyone a lot of money to go through. Okay, Mom? And guess what? Beanie got her fortune told and got lost in the Haunted House."

"Thanks, dweeb," Beanie said, glaring at Jerm.

"Don't mention it," he replied, beaming.

He jumped up and started a rap song. "You stink, you stink. You know it."

"What do you need for your Haunted House, Jerm?" Mrs. Kingsley asked tactfully.

Jerm plopped down on the piano bench, his little performance finished. "Eyeballs," he said happily. "A lot of 'em. And bats, real ones from the woods. Maybe some mashed-up oatmeal. Oh! A chain saw."

"What?" Beanie squealed. "A chain saw? That's gross."

"And I'm going to put up a bunch of shower curtains to block your view as you go through. And have sound effects. It's going to be awesome."

Instead of leaping up to go help him start this new project, as she once would have, Mrs. Kingsley simply smiled and said, "Sounds great, Jerm. But first, I want to tell you something. You know I had a doctor's appointment this afternoon? And we talked about how my muscles ache, and my fever, and how I have to rest a lot right now?"

Beanie and Jerm glanced at each other. Jerm began slowly writing his name in the dust on the keyboard cover.

"Well, I got the results of the tests I had done last week. They didn't show anything wrong—isn't that great? So it's possible I have something called CFS, Chronic Fatigue Syndrome. It's a disease that often gives me a low fever. It slows me down. Sometimes it makes my muscles jerky and hard to control."

"Remember that time you couldn't talk or walk right? What about that?" Beanie said.

"I did ask him. He said just to rest more, not to push too hard. Otherwise, it's not all that serious," Mrs. Kingsley said.

"That's all?" said Jerm cheerfully. "We knew that already."

CFS not serious? It seemed serious. Her mom hadn't been able to work in months. If she didn't rest a lot, her fever got worse.

Having a fever was terrible. And having an incurable disease forever and ever didn't seem like something to smile and act reassuring about. Her mom was saying these things so they wouldn't worry. In reality, it seemed foggy and horrible—just as Madame Olivia had said.

"Mom, did you find out if there's any medicine for you to take? At least for the fever?" Beanie asked.

"Honey, they don't know what causes this. The doctor said he doesn't even believe in it. Now, about that friendly fortune-teller. Let me tell you something. I don't need a fortune-teller—I am one."

"You are?" Jerm looked stunned.

"Mom!" Beanie knew her mom was intentionally changing the subject. She felt annoyed that her mother was trying to cheer them up by fooling around.

"I am Madame Squidley, the All-Knowing."

"Squidley?" Beanie smiled in spite of herself. "Nice name."

"You don't know everything, Mom," Jerm scoffed.

"Yes, I do. For example, I know that Beanie got upset at the carnival."

Jerm glanced at his sister. "Yeah. How did you know that?" he asked.

"The All-Knowing One is infinitely wise."

Beanie barely heard her. It was awful, her mom being sick. And there was no one to help out. Their Uncle Ozzy and Auntie Jane had adopted two little girls from China and had no room for Beanie and Jerm, and Auntie Jane complained about the laundry as it was, without having two more kids to wash for.

So what would happen if their mom got worse? What if she had to go into the hospital? Who would take care of them? Would Uncle Ozzy fly here? Beanie wished she knew exactly what would happen. The uncertainty kept her on edge.

Beanie felt tears well up in her eyes. She and Jerm would be homeless then, and nobody would care. Unless—this was the spark of hope that glowed in her chest—Mrs. Adams came for them and said they could live with her family, at her house. Fretfully, Beanie started to chew her thumbnail, even though it was already so short that it was hard for her teeth to get ahold of.

"So did Dr. Howell say anything about your job?" Beanie asked. Mrs. Kingsley was a paralegal for a large law firm in Portland.

"Oh, he said I can go back anytime. When school reopens, I thought I'd start again," her mother answered.

"Can somebody there help you?" Jerm asked.

"Help me? No, no one would have time for that," Mrs. Kingsley said.

When she and Beanie had first become ill, Mrs. Kingsley's work friends had brought them flowers and casseroles and CDs to listen to. But after a month, everyone drifted away. Nobody lived in Weymouth, and the distance of the drive to and from Portland was enough of an obstacle to keep people from popping in.

"And what about our trip to Loon Lake?" Beanie

asked eagerly. "Are we going? We are, aren't we? It's almost Labor Day weekend."

Her mother looked down and sighed. "I'm sorry, Beanie, Jerm. I don't think we should go this year. I want to save my energy for starting work and—"

"Oh. Yeah, that's okay," Beanie said. "Right, Jerm?"

"Yeah. We can go another time."

"Listen, Jerm. Why don't I tell your fortune?"

"Now you're talking, Squidley."

"First, however, I shall head-butt Beanie in the belly."

"Mom!" Beanie squealed helplessly as her mom gently butted her, whispering, "Don't worry, sweetie pie. Let's give this some more time, all right? I can still take perfectly good care of you. He said I won't get worse. I probably just won't get better for a while. And I'm sorry about the camping trip."

"It's okay." But Beanie felt a shiver run through her. She thought about losing her dad when she was in nursery school. And now this . . . very sorrowful fog. She hated Dr. Howell for not helping them today. Didn't he understand how bad things were for her mom? How exhausted she was? How dizzy and pale she got?

Her mother *was* really sick, no matter what the doctor said. Beanie couldn't help comparing her to Mrs. Adams, who always looked so strong and healthy. The Adamses went to the Bahamas for February vacation every year and came back with tans. Mrs. Kingsley couldn't even sit in the bright sunlight. And everyone—all the girls at school, anyway—liked Miranda. Right now only Charles Sprague and Jerm liked Beanie. Well, there was also Ernestine Brown. But she was such a pain and so absolutely weird that she didn't count.

"Come on. Tell my fortune, Squidley." Jerm was hopping up and down, nearly beside himself with impatience.

Beanie's mother cocked her head to one side. "Is that any way to speak to the keen-sighted and mysterious Madame Squidley?"

Jerm clasped his hands behind his back. "No," he said. "Madame Squidley, please can you tell my fortune? Please?"

"Ah. Better. Well, I might possibly, for a slight fee, that is," Mrs. Kingsley replied. "Empty your pockets, Mr. Moneybags."

"That's no fair, Mom. You're looking for clues," Beanie said.

"I'm not," she answered as Jerm brought out gum wrappers, a stone, a paper clip, and some lint. "I was hoping to be paid for my very difficult work. But never mind. This wad of lint will do as a token of appreciation. Thank you. Okay, Jeremiah Kingsley. No crystal ball for me. Go bring me—let me see. Ah, yes. Go bring me an onion."

Jerm raced for one and brought it to her.

"Very good. Now sit down while I peer deeply into

my malodorous yet mystical onion. But I gotta tell you, after I do this, Madame Squidley will have to rest again before dinner."

Jerm asked, "Didn't you rest already?"

"Yes, but today Squidley is extra tired. Now hush. The mighty onion speaks! It says that Jerm is like a seed waiting to find a garden. Eaten by a bird, carried through the air in the bird's stomach, and then dropped out the bird's other end into a farmer's field—"

"Mom! That's no fortune," Jerm interrupted.

"Oh, dear! The onion hates interruptions. Sorry. Contact with the Unknown has vanished."

With that, Mrs. Kingsley went into the kitchen and lay down on a small sofa. From there she could supervise as Beanie cooked dinner.

5

BEANIE WAS IN CHARGE OF PREPARING THE TOMATO sauce. She took the magic onion and put it on the cutting board. She hated cooking dinner, but with her mother tired nearly every afternoon, she had to learn how.

She rummaged through the kitchen drawer, looking for a knife that was sharp but not too sharp.

Jerm got out the big frying pan and set it on the stove. He was the supply man.

Beanie held the onion still and tried to slice it down the middle. The outside peels of the onion were brown and slippery and surprisingly hard. The onion squirted out of her hand and rolled across the counter. "Get over here," she muttered. She frowned and gripped the onion more firmly.

"Beanie, just a second," said her mom. "Make sure you know where your fingers are before you press down on that knife."

"Of course I know where my fingers are."

"Okay, okay. I don't always. That's why I mentioned it." She held up a bandaged index finger that

Beanie knew she had cut slicing red peppers two days before.

"Who got cut with a knife? You, Mom?" Jerm said brightly, sliding across the kitchen linoleum in his socks. "Can I see?"

As far as Beanie was concerned, Jerm was a colossal annoyance with a special sense for zeroing in on crises. Band-Aids interested him. He often wore them on his knees or across his nose. He even had a Band-Aid collection (unused): Fred Flintstone, Scooby-Doo, the Dalmatians, plus special medical ones such as the butterfly strip.

Annoyed, Beanie said, "Can I have some privacy around here? I'm slicing an onion, that's all. So just . . . just . . . whatever."

Her mother leaned against the pillow, hugging Jerm to her side, anchoring him. "You can watch with me. Beanie, may I make another suggestion?"

"I guess so," Beanie muttered.

"It's a whole lot easier to cut the onion open if you peel off that slippery brown skin first."

"I knew that," Jerm piped up.

Finally Beanie sliced the onion more or less down the middle and peered into the center. There was nothing particularly interesting inside. Just layer after layer of wet, white onion rings packed together. No place for magic powers.

"Pfew! Wow. It smells." Beanie rinsed the onion juice off her hands at the sink. Her eyes were starting to sting.

"Here," her mom said. "I'll chop it for you. Bring me the cutting board."

"It's all yours, Madame Squidley," Beanie answered.

Beanie dumped the chopped onion into the frying pan and added a jar of tomato sauce to simmer. Just then, Charles banged on the back door and came in. Buckled around his waist like a very wide plastic belt was the brace for his scoliosis. The brace helped his spine stay straight instead of curving like a long letter S. His mother believed that the brace would help if he wore it enough, but his dad, a crane operator at the shipyard in Bath, thought the brace was useless and that playing sports was the way to straighten his spine.

"Hey, guys. It's time for four square again. Let the games begin! Mrs. Kingsley, can you play, too?"

"Sure," said Beanie's mother, sitting up.

"Mom, I thought you had to rest before dinner. Besides, don't you think it might be too hot today for you?" Beanie asked worriedly. Her mom got extra pale and shaky when it was hot.

"No, no, I'll be fine. Let's do it, guys. The spaghetti sauce can simmer while we play."

So out they went. The squares had been drawn in blue chalk in the middle of the road. They played there, since no one ever drove down Poplar Lane except the residents and occasional delivery trucks. The boxes were numbered one through four. Number one was the server's box. Four was the entry box, where you were sent if you failed to return the ball properly.

"Just so you know, Charles, I have a new Four Square Federation name for myself," Mrs. Kingsley said, while Jerm hunted in their shed for the ball.

"Yeah?"

"It's Madame Squidley."

"She thinks she's a fortune-teller," Beanie explained.

"She doesn't think, she knows," her mother said.

They had crazy names for playing four square. Beanie was Killer Bee, and Charles was Splat. Miranda was Peachfuzz, but she almost never played. Jerm didn't have a name yet because every time someone suggested a name for him, he rejected it.

"I can't find the ball!" Jerm hollered from the shed.

"Keep looking," Madame Squidley yelled back through cupped hands.

"The lines are a little faded. I'll get a new piece of chalk so we can redraw them," Beanie said, racing back inside.

She opened a large drawer in the china cupboard. They called it the Drawer of Chaos, and it was filled with such useful things as superglue, duct tape, whistles, kazoos, bubble-blowing liquid, food coloring, dice, balloons, telephone wire, batteries, and chalk.

Beanie grabbed the chalk, ran back outside, and carefully redrew the lines. And finally Jerm found the ball.

"On your mark, get set," called Charles. "Here goes."

Charles served a low one to Beanie, the Killer Bee. She lunged for it, returning it to Jerm. The ball bounced once in his box, then hit his sneaker and careened off into the tall, unmowed grass in Charles's yard. That was the end of that volley.

"Go get the ball, Jerm," Beanie said.

"No." He sat down in his box, pouting. Beanie glanced at her mom to see what she would say to Jeremiah, but she was bent forward, her hands resting on her knees, her face pale in a way that worried Beanie whenever she saw it.

"I don't have a name yet and summer's almost over," Jerm said. "I don't want to play without a name."

"Holy cow," muttered Beanie.

Charles laughed. "Yeah, how about Holy Cow for a name?"

"Mom," whined Jerm.

"Are you speaking to Madame Squidley?" Mrs. Kingsley said. "Go get the ball while I, the All-Knowing, think of a name."

Jerm scrambled to his feet and retrieved the ball from the tall grass near the Spragues' driveway. The Kingsleys never mowed their lawn, either. The two yards looked more like meadows for cows. Both houses could have used a fresh coat of paint, as well.

"Madame Squidley has chosen a name for Jeremiah."

"Well, what is it?" Jerm asked.

"Jump. Your Four Square Federation name is Jump."

"Jump?" asked Jerm doubtfully. "That sounds like a kangaroo. How about . . . Rump. That's better."

"Rump!" Charles howled.

Beanie joined in his laughter. Soon they were both overcome and barely able to stand.

Jerm glared at them. "What's so funny?" he asked. "Rump is a good name. I like it."

"Rump is a place kind of near your backside," Charles said, laughing helplessly.

"Mom," Jerm protested.

"They are a bit immature, aren't they?" Madame Squidley said. "Serve 'em up, Splat. Let's go."

So Splat served the ball to Madame Squidley. She tapped it to Rump, who hit it with his forearm but still managed to get it into Killer Bee's box. Once they got into a rhythm, they finally managed to get some good volleys going.

Then it was Madame Squidley's turn in the server's box. She wiped the sweat from her forehead and bounced the ball a few times first. Beanie watched her mom carefully, waiting for the serve. But it didn't come. Instead, her mother seemed to weave a little on her feet.

"Mom?" Beanie asked.

Her mother's eyes closed for a moment. She didn't answer.

"Are you okay?" Charles asked.

"Just tired," Mrs. Kingsley said. "I feel a little . . ."

Beanie hurried over and took the ball. "Maybe you should go inside now," she said.

"Yeah," her mother said faintly, as though she were half asleep.

But instead of going into the house, she sat down abruptly at the edge of the road. Her face was chalky white. Even her lips were pale. Beanie took her mother's hand. It felt icy cold, but now her cheeks turned bright red.

"Are you hot or cold?" Beanie asked.

"Hot," her mother answered. "I think."

"Should I go get my mom?" Charles asked Beanie in a low voice. "Although she'd probably become hysterical."

"No. It's just the heat and her legs. Sort of. They get weak or something if she stands up too much. She needs a cold washcloth. That usually helps a lot," Beanie said. "Jerm, sit here next to her. You too, Charles. I'll be right back."

Moments later, Beanie came out with a wet dish towel and knelt by her mother. "Here, Mom," she said, putting the dish towel in her mother's hands.

Mrs. Kingsley held the cold towel to the sides of her face and neck. "Oh, that's such a help. Thanks, Beanie," she said, her words much less blurry.

"She still sounds kind of slowed down and funny," Charles said. "I think I should go get my mom."

"No. This happens when she's overtired or overheated or something."

"Wait. Look! There's a car turning the corner. An SUV!" Jerm shouted. "Hey!" he yelled, waving his arms. "It's Mrs. Adams. Hey! Hurry up!"

"Jerm, don't yell," Beanie said. "God."

But she waved, too, and the SUV stopped. Mrs. Adams jumped out and walked quickly to where Mrs. Kingsley sat at the edge of the road. The SUV side door opened and Miranda climbed out as well.

"What happened here?" Mrs. Adams asked, crouching down.

"We were playing four square, and she got too tired and had to stop. And Beanie brought Mom a cold wet towel," Jerm said. "And that helped. And then you came."

"I wasn't feeling too well today," murmured Mrs. Kingsley.

"You shouldn't be out here playing with the kids in this heat, Nora."

"I asked her to," Beanie said protectively.

"Yeah, me too," Charles said. "We dragged her out of the house. It's our fault."

"What do you want me to do, Nora? Can I help you get inside? Goodness, you're hot. Do you have a fever?"

"I don't know. Probably," Mrs. Kingsley said. "It comes and goes."

Charles's mother rushed out. "What's going on? What's going on?" Mrs. Sprague called.

"Oh, no," Charles muttered.

"Should I call the rescue? Is Nora okay?" Mrs.

Sprague came flapping down the driveway in flip-flops, shorts, and an enormous lime-green T-shirt.

"Don't call anybody, Celeste," Mrs. Adams said. "She just needs to go inside and lie down. Here. Take her other arm."

Slowly they helped Mrs. Kingsley to her feet, Miranda still hanging back and Beanie running ahead to open the door. With support, Mrs. Kingsley walked into the kitchen. Mrs. Adams led her to the small sofa, then got her a glass of cold water. Beanie was relieved that the neighbors had rushed to help.

"Thank you," Beanie's mother said gratefully. "I was at the doctor's today. I guess I got a little overtired."

"Well, what did he say? You haven't been feeling well for months now," Mrs. Adams said.

"They didn't find anything major wrong. He said it was probably Chronic Fatigue Syndrome, from when Beanie and I had the flu last April. Parts of the immune system stay switched on, and it causes a cascade of symptoms." Then she smiled. "And the doctor said that I should rest as much as possible, but he also said I should exercise as much as possible. So take your pick."

"Oh, for heaven's sake. Doctors can be so annoying. Doesn't he understand this is a real problem? You need more to go on than that!" said Mrs. Adams. "Here, Beanie, run some more cool water on this dish towel for your mom. Is there someone we can call?

Someone who can come stay here with you? I hate to leave you and the kids alone like this."

"Charles and I are just across the street if you need anything, Nora," Mrs. Sprague said.

"No, no. We'll be fine."

Mrs. Adams said, "Well, you're not fine now. Listen, Nora, why don't we have Beanie over tonight for a sleepover? That's a nice idea, isn't it, Miranda?"

Miranda didn't answer right away. The whole time she had stood in the doorway, watching the scene with a sulky look on her face.

"Oh. I guess so. Come on over whenever, Beanie. I was going to watch a Tom Cruise movie. You can watch it with me."

Beanie and Charles glanced at each other. Charles, the movie buff, held his nose to show Beanie what he thought of Tom Cruise. Beanie held back a giggle.

"Okay, Miranda. Thanks. I'll come over around seven-thirty." Beanie handed her mom another cool towel for her face and neck.

Miranda turned toward Charles. "So, are you going to have to wear that thing to school?" she asked.

"Miranda!" Mrs. Adams said sharply.

"No, it's okay. It's not a 'thing,' " Charles said. "It's my back brace. For curvature of the spine. Scoliosis."

"We call it his car seat," Beanie said to amuse Miranda. But when she looked closely at Miranda, she was surprised to see that Miranda's eyelids were red and puffy.

"No we don't," said Charles angrily. "Shut up, Beanie. Anyway, I'm not wearing it to school."

As the Adamses got back in their SUV, Beanie wondered if Miranda had been crying.

"Come on, Charles," Mrs. Sprague said.

"Yeah, okay. Just think, Beanie, if you survive this sleepover, you might become a member of the Snob Squad. Your dream come true," said Charles.

Beanie gave an embarrassed laugh. She felt bad for teasing Charles in front of Miranda, but what he'd said was true—she was desperately hoping she could be part of the in crowd this year. Maybe that way she could turn her unsuccessful life around.

Maybe, if tonight went well, then the next time Barbie had a sleepover, Beanie'd be invited to that, too. Then she'd be in the Snob Squad for sure because Barbie was its queen.

"Bye now," Charles said. "Hope you feel better, Squidley."

"Thank you, Splat. You're a good friend," Mrs. Kingsley said.

"But, Charles! I want you to help me make a Haunted House," Jerm wailed. "Hey, while Beanie's at the sleepover tonight, we can work on it in the basement, okay?"

"Yeah. Sure. I'll help you. Are you charging money to go through it?"

"Yeah. Two dollars."

Charles hooted with laughter.

"One dollar for each of us," Jerm added.

Beanie felt a pang. There was nearly always something exciting going on at her house. Tonight she would miss it.

Jerm picked up his clipboard from the kitchen counter. "When you get home, look for stuff, okay? We need plastic tablecloths, olives, cold spaghetti, lights, black construction paper. And sound effects like screams and stuff. Do you have a black widow spider or anything like that? Any bats?"

"No. But I'll bring the olives and some sound effects on tape my mom has for drama. See you later," Charles said as he left.

Making the Haunted House sounded like fun, much more fun than sitting around with sulky Miranda and watching a Tom Cruise movie. But Beanie had to go. And if she had to break off her friendship with Charles in order to hang out with Miranda, then she would.

Beanie raced for the rope hammock under the trees in the backyard, her favorite place for daydreaming and reading. She flopped into the hammock stomach first and stared at the ground.

Never mind the Haunted House, she told herself. Finally she could do something more mature than sitting around rereading her favorite books, or feeding Charles's pet tortoise chocolate ice cream, or watching Boris Karloff movies.

And then she thought about her mom, turning so pale and sinking weakly to the ground. Beanie had been hoping the doctor would give her mom a pill or a shot or something. Then her mother could go back to being the way she'd always been—hilarious and full of surprises and ready to play. Not the way she was now, a pale ghost of a person who couldn't even push the grocery cart through the store by herself. I just want my real mom back, Beanie thought. And she started to cry.

6

Mrs. Adams let Beanie in. As usual, Mr. Adams was away on business. Beanie climbed the stairs to Miranda's room, admiring the white-carpeted steps, even though they made her sneakers look worn and dusty by contrast.

Miranda's bedroom door was open. "Hi, Beanie. Come on in. I'll start the movie in a minute. It's *Jerry Maguire*. I've seen it before, so we don't have to watch every second of it."

Beanie hadn't seen it, but she didn't say so. She didn't want Miranda to think she was completely out of it. Miranda slid the disc into the DVD player and clicked it on. Then she pulled Clue from under her bed.

"I love this game," said Miranda. "But I absolutely have to be Miss Scarlet."

Beanie pressed her lips together. "Clue takes forever."

"No, it doesn't. Come on. Pick a person so we can get started."

For a beginning fifth grader, Miranda Adams was very grownup and stylish. Long-legged, she had curly ash-blond hair that her mother let her streak with hair dye from the pharmacy. She plucked her eyebrows with tweezers, and this summer she had been a counselor-in-training for the five- and six-year-olds at the recreation department day camp, for three whole weeks.

Beanie and Miranda had been playing for nearly forty minutes. Beanie was Colonel Mustard and Miranda, naturally, was Miss Scarlet. Beanie was just narrowing in on a weapon (she thought it was the lead pipe) and suspect (she suspected herself) when Miranda suddenly announced, "Let's not finish this now. Here. I'll push the game board under my bed. We can finish later. I want to show you what I bought with Barbie this morning, before the fair."

Then Miranda went to her huge closet, opened the louvered doors, pulled out the school clothes she had bought on the shopping trip, and piled them on her bed. Two pairs of tight Capri pants. Earrings. New sneakers. A black track suit. Clogs. A new L.L. Bean backpack. Beanie smiled and smiled, but inside she slowly felt worse and worse, a weird kind of pressure building up in her chest and throat.

"But you know what? I have to return the earrings," Miranda said bitterly.

"Why?"

"Oh, because . . . my mother is such an idiot."

"No, she's not. Your mother is wonderful. She won that tennis championship last spring, remember?"

"So what? Who cares about some tennis trophy?"

Beanie inspected the earrings. They were made of

tiny beads of amber and green glass. "These are nice," she said. "Why are you taking them back?"

"Because my mom thinks I shoplifted them."

"What? Did you?" Beanie stared at her.

"Yes," admitted Miranda. "But don't tell anybody. I'm trusting you not to tell, Beanie."

"I won't. I promise. But why did you do that?"

"Barbie does it sometimes. Just little stuff like candy. She does it a lot, actually. Anyway, she told me to put these in my pocket. So I did. My mom knew something was up, but she didn't actually see me do it."

"Wow," Beanie said again. "But I still don't get why you're mad at your mom."

"Because. When we got to the car, she made me show them to her, and she yelled at us. Then she called Barbie's house and told her mother about it. And when we got home, she called the store! Can you imagine how embarrassed and awful I'm going to feel when I go back to the store tomorrow? Why can't she just forget about it? I said I was sorry. Plus, I didn't feel like having a guest over tonight. I just wanted to be left alone. She's always bossing me around."

"Oh," Beanie said awkwardly. She sat down on the edge of the bed, shocked to discover that all was not well in the Adams household. Miranda had stolen the earrings, but instead of feeling apologetic, she was angry with her mother! And she was being rude to Beanie, too, making her feel unwelcome. She'd never realized that Miranda was so dishonest.

In third grade, she and Miranda had been best friends. In fourth grade, at the end of the year, Miranda teamed up with Barbie. She'd still talked with Beanie on the bus, but that was it.

Beanie wanted to go home to the safety, warmth, and silliness of her own home. Instead, a long night in a sleeping bag on Miranda's bedroom floor loomed before her.

There was a tap on the door.

"Yoo-hoo. Coming in."

Mrs. Adams had brought them little snack pizzas on a tray, which she set down between them. Next to the flowery paper plates, she had placed a small vase with a single red rosebud in it, and there were flowery paper napkins. Beanie's mother couldn't even carry a tray upstairs without feeling tired and wobbly afterward. Beanie knew she shouldn't compare her mother to Mrs. Adams, but she couldn't seem to stop.

"Thanks, Mrs. Adams," Beanie said appreciatively. "How pretty."

Beanie stared at the screen. At this point, Tom Cruise was moving out, leaving behind a cute little boy and his mom. Beanie looked away abruptly. She set the paper plate with the small pizza on the floor, pressed her hands over her eyes, and squeezed her face into a tight grimace. She didn't want to see anything sad or scary today.

"Beanie, dear, are you all right?" Mrs. Adams asked, stooping down beside her, stroking her hair.

"Yeah," she muttered. "I'm okay."

"Are you worried about your mom?"

"I guess so." She didn't want Miranda to notice she was almost crying.

"Maybe we can try to—" Mrs. Adams began.

"Mom! Not now. Show time!" Miranda interrupted.

Mrs. Adams straightened up. "Enjoy the movie, girls. Beanie, we can talk another time."

"Isn't Tom Cruise adorable?" Miranda asked when her mother had left.

"Umm-hmm, he really is," Beanie echoed lamely.

The movie ended around nine-thirty, and they turned the lights off at eleven. But Beanie lay awake in her sleeping bag on the hard floor, staring up at the dark ceiling. She couldn't keep her eyes closed for even ten minutes. She didn't want to have a cloudy future. Why had the fortune-teller said such a mean thing to her? Why hadn't she said that Beanie would be a world-class gymnast? Or someone who photographed polar bears and penguins?

Didn't Miranda realize that she had a perfect life? Besides cooking, Beanie often had to do a lot of housework, too—vacuuming, laundry, sweeping, scrubbing. Jerm had to dust and take out the garbage. Miranda didn't have to do anything. Beanie wished they had a cleaning lady, the way the Adamses did.

The Adamses had a lawn care service come and mow their impressively green grass, which they watered with an underground sprinkler system. But even with that smooth grass, Miranda had shoplifted a pair of earrings. Beanie sighed and tried to think of something else. She felt hot and sweaty in the sleeping bag, which was designed to keep you warm down to twenty below zero. Beanie didn't feel comfortable here at all. She wanted to be home, in her own bed, with her own mom nearby.

When she turned over restlessly, the sleeping bag tangled and twisted around her legs. She looked at Miranda's alarm clock. Twelve o'clock came. Then one.

Beanie couldn't stand lying awake another minute. She unzipped the bag, slid her legs out, and tiptoed to Miranda's bed. "Miranda? Hey. Wake up. You know what? I have to go home. I can't sleep."

"What?" Miranda asked sleepily, lifting her head off the pillow. "Go home now? Beanie, it's the middle of the night."

"Well, yeah. I know." But you didn't even want to have me over in the first place, Beanie wanted to add. Already she was pulling sneakers on her bare feet.

"You're going home in your pj's?" Miranda asked.

"Yeah. You can watch out the window and make sure I get there. Tell your mom I had a stomachache or something."

Miranda sat up, her ash-blond curls mussed from the pillow. "I can't believe this. Boy, Beanie. It's one o'clock in the morning! You really hurt my feelings."

"I didn't mean to, Miranda. Really, I didn't," Beanie mumbled miserably. "But I gotta go. See ya."

In her pajamas and untied sneakers, carrying her bunched-up sleeping bag and clothes, Beanie stumbled out of Miranda's house and hurried down the dark street. She opened her back door, which they never locked, day or night, let herself inside, and tiptoed barefoot up the stairs, hoping that Miranda would never tell the kids at school that she was a big baby.

Beanie turned on the light in her room and slipped off her sneakers. She glanced at her alarm clock. Nearly one-thirty.

"Beanie?" Her mother stood in the doorway. "What's up?"

"Oh. Hi."

"Why did you come home, sweetie? Is anything wrong?"

"I couldn't sleep."

"No? Here. Lie down now. I'll rub your back with baby powder to cool you off."

Beanie stretched out on her bed. Her mother turned off the light. The familiar darkness of Beanie's room felt comforting.

"Mom? Can you go to a different doctor? One that can help you get better? There has to be one."

"Well," her mother said slowly, "the problem is that there's nothing anyone can really do. Some doctors think people who have CFS aren't really sick at all, that they're just exaggerating the pain and fatigue."

"What?" said Beanie angrily, struggling to sit up.

Her mom laughed. "Hey, take it easy!"

"That's so mean. Isn't there someone else you can ask—"

"No. Please, Beanie. Try to get some sleep." Her

mother stood up. "Time for that overactive brain to rest."

"What about your overactive brain?" Beanie asked. "Can't you sleep?"

"Me? No. For some very annoying reason, I can hardly sleep at all now. But we'll talk about it tomorrow, Beanie. That's enough for today."

"G'night. Love you," Beanie murmured.

7

"HOW WAS THE SLEEPOVER?" CHARLES ASKED AS he let Beanie in at ten the next morning.

"Terrible."

"Ha. How is it I'm not surprised?"

"I don't know. I don't care right now. We have to find my mom another doctor, Charles. But how?"

"Calm down, Beanie. Don't panic, or you'll end up like my mom. Why don't you just call your mom's doctor and ask him for the name of someone else? Maybe another doctor can help. That's what we did with my scoliosis. We got a second opinion."

"Call the doctor? Me?"

"Yeah. We can call from here. I'll dial the phone for you right now."

"Really? You think it's okay?"

"Yeah. Ask him stuff. What is it you want to know? How come there's no medicine or operations. Anything else?"

"Is she going to get worse or what? She said she's not, but she might just be saying that so I won't worry."

"Now, let's see. His name is Dr. Howell?" Charles asked, looking in the gray pages.

"Yep. Howell."

"Here it is. Leo R. Howell. Okay. Give me the phone."

Beanie wiped her sweaty palms on the seat of her shorts while Charles punched in the numbers. Then he handed her the receiver.

"Umm. Hello. I need to talk to Dr. Howell. This is Beatrice Kingsley. It's very, extremely urgent."

"Urgent? Very extremely?" asked Charles.

"Shut up, Charles."

He crawled over to the sofa and pulled his tortoise out of the shadows. The tortoise's legs pawed the air as Charles turned him upside down.

"Hello, Mr. Turtley Wurtley. How are you today?" Charles said.

"I'm on hold," Beanie whispered. "They're playing elevator music." She held the phone out so Charles could hear. "I Could Have Danced All Night, dah dah, dee dee, dah dahhhhh."

"Cool."

Charles gave her the thumbs up. He set Mr. Turtley Wurtley on the floor. Immediately the tortoise began to crawl toward the bathroom, heaving himself along on his short claws to where his lettuce, turtle food, and water were kept.

"Hi. Is this Dr. Howell? I'm Nora Kingsley's kid, her daughter . . . And I'm ten actually, not that little."

Charles clapped his hand over his mouth, as if to stifle a giggle.

"The reason I called is I want to know why you can't help my mom. It's really not fair to tell her there's nothing you can do. I mean that's your job, right? To help people? She is sick. Really. You don't understand!" Beanie felt tears choking her voice.

"Well, Miss Kingsley," said Dr. Howell, "I didn't mean to be unfair when I said that. It's just that medically we have no idea what causes the problems your mother is having, so we really have no way of helping her. It's as simple as that. I'm very sorry."

He sounded nicer than Beanie had expected.

"But I don't want her to have to be like this!" Beanie said. "She can't play with us or anything. Not like she did before. And she forgets stuff. She forgets everything, even what day it is. She couldn't remember your name. And she can't sleep at all. I want her to go to another doctor. Some brand-new doctor maybe would know what to do."

"I don't know if you understand. If she indeed has a disease, there has to be a cause. But in all our tests, we found nothing out of the ordinary. I'm not sure that another doctor could help. May I ask you if she knows you called me?"

"No. I mean, she doesn't know. She told me she'd be okay and not to worry. But she's not okay at all. She can't even go to work," Beanie said in a discouraged voice. "And I have to cook dinner nearly every night."

"Again, I apologize for not being able to help her. But I don't think another doctor is the answer."

"But sometimes it helps?"

"Well, yes. If someone has a rare form of cancer. Or severe diabetes. Or blindness or perhaps a brain tumor, but we've ruled those physical things out now and—"

"Oh. Well, then. That's okay. Thanks." Beanie didn't want to hear about any more awful diseases. There were so many! "I guess I better go now. Bye, Dr. Howell. Thank you."

"You're very welcome, young lady."

She hung up. "He said I was very welcome," she told Charles.

"But what else did he say? No second opinion?" Charles asked.

Beanie shook her head. "He doesn't think that would help. You know what we need? Someone to come help do chores."

Together they stood in the bathroom doorway and watched Mr. Turtley Wurtley rip apart a wilted shred of lettuce with his tough little beak.

"Summer's almost over," Charles said finally.

"Yeah."

"Labor Day weekend's coming up. I have to go to my dad's house. What are you guys doing?"

"Us? For Labor Day? I don't know. The last two years, we went to Loon Lake campground. It was really fun."

"Are you going this year?"

"I don't know. Well, I do know. No," Beanie said softly.

She and Jerm had loved camping out by the lake with a view of the mountains of New Hampshire rising up, blue in the distance. They went to sleep at night listening to the loons calling one another, their warbling voices like drops of silvery liquid. Tears of disappointment stung her eyes.

"Can we change the subject? What do you think Miss Bennett will be like, anyway?" Beanie asked.

"I don't know. She's new. I hope we get to do a play."

"You want to be an actor?"

"No, I want to be the sound and lights director."

Beanie thought that a play might be fun, but she was barely paying attention. If the doctor couldn't help, how *was* she supposed to manage? How could she possibly take care of her mom, go to school, play with Jerm and Charles, and do chores galore? What kind of life was that?

She said goodbye to Charles and wandered off to swing in the hammock. This time she didn't pretend that Mrs. Adams was her mom. She wanted to think about something quite real, a way for Jerm, Beanie, and her mom to get some help.

⌒

School was starting on Wednesday, September 6, ready or not. Beanie planned to spend her last few days of freedom swinging in the hammock, rereading *The*

Wonderful Wizard of Oz, playing Monopoly, which was Jerm's favorite game because he wanted to be a millionaire in real life, playing poker, which was Charles's favorite game because gangsters always played it in old movies, or playing four square, which was her favorite game.

With Charles's help, Jerm opened his Haunted House on Friday. Beanie was their first victim. She paid two dollars and took off her sneakers, as instructed. The boys put a blindfold (Charles's old Cub Scout scarf) over her eyes, then turned on the tape deck with the scary-music cassette. Jerm was the leader, and Charles, hiding somewhere among the shower curtains, was the special-effects man. Beanie heard a chain clanking and the rasp of a saw on wood.

"Do you hear that sound?" cackled Jerm. "Heee-heeeheee!"

"Which one?" Beanie asked.

"That saw is going to saw off your bones."

"Is that a fact?" Beanie said.

"Beanie! You have to be scared!" Jerm said. "Come on."

"Okay, okay. I'm scared. Don't have a hissy fit."

Jerm led her forward. "First you must walk through a—a— Charles, I forget what the spaghetti is."

"Oh, great," Beanie muttered, trying not to giggle.

"Cat intestines," Charles said from behind the curtains. "With mutated eyeballs mixed in."

Jerm directed Beanie to step into a pan of what she knew was cooked spaghetti with cold olives in it.

"This is absolutely disgusting," she said. "Jerm, get me out of here."

"There's a towel on the other side."

Quickly Beanie stepped out of the muck and onto a dry towel. She heard a crescendo of organ music, and again Jerm cackled. Then the shower curtains flapped and what felt like a rubber chicken swatted her in the face.

"Once you enter here, you'll never escape. This was old McDonald's farm, but the animals are dead now . . ." Jerm said in his deepest voice.

Beanie had had enough. She wanted the blindfold off. She didn't want anyone pulling her through gooey, cold stuff. She gritted her teeth, not wanting to be a disappointing victim.

"Now. Sit here in this chair, old lady. While you've been in the Haunted House, you have aged. You are old and wrinkly. So very, very old." Jerm pushed her backward, and she sat down right on a whoopee cushion that let out a loud, rubbery blat of air.

"Aaaaah!" Beanie screamed, jumping to her feet. She slipped on the plastic tablecloth and fell abruptly, landing on her backside.

Jerm laughed hysterically. Beanie ripped the blindfold off. "I'm not doing this, you guys. Get somebody else for your Haunted House."

She flung the Cub Scout scarf into the wet

spaghetti and stomped off upstairs for a proper sulk in her bedroom. This was exactly why she couldn't be expected to hang around with Charles and Jerm all her life. They were intolerable. They were disgusting.

She needed girl friends who would always take her side, help her with her problems, go shopping with her. If that meant she had to join the Snob Squad, then that's what she'd have to do. Even if Barbie and Miranda did some things that were wrong, she still dreamed of being part of their group. She had to make her move this year, in fifth grade.

8

SCHOOL STARTED ON A HOT AND STEAMY WED-
nesday. A tropical storm lurked somewhere off the
coast, funneling a mass of thick humidity into Maine.
At Weymouth Elementary School, with its flat, gravel-
covered roof, the classrooms were unbearably hot.

Charles, Miranda, Barbie, and Beanie were in Miss
Bennett's class. Ernestine had Mr. Woodward, thank
goodness. This was Miss Bennett's first teaching as-
signment, and she looked as young as a high school
student.

"Now, I want you to look at my star chart," she
said. "Stars will be awarded to anyone going above
and beyond what's expected—doing extra-credit work,
picking up after class, volunteering. The most important thing is community service, how you treat others."

Beanie yawned. She was having trouble concentrat-
ing. How you treat others. Teachers had no idea how
kids actually treated one another. How Barbie called
her "piggy nose," for example. Yet Barbie would probably be the first one to get a star, because she was such
a kiss-up.

Beanie laid her head on the desk. She wondered how her mom was doing on her first day back at work. Worrying was so tiring. She yawned again.

"Miss Kingsley? Are you awake?"

Beanie sat up. "Yes." She glanced at Charles, and he waggled his eyebrows at her to make her smile.

"Everyone's books should be covered by tomorrow. You don't have to buy covers. Paper bags will do. Just get it done, boys and girls."

When they were dismissed for morning recess, the Snob Squad girls crowded around the new teacher, admiring her clothes and shoes. Beanie hurried over and tried to join them. She edged her way in near Miranda.

"Hi," Beanie said, still trying to squeeze her body into the tight circle of girls. Meanwhile, Barbie moved closer to Miranda on the other side.

"Beanie! Cut it out. Quit pushing!" Miranda said.

"Yeah. Get out of here, Bean-Geek," Barbie whispered. "Go play with your baby brother. Or your boyfriend, Charles Sprague."

"He's not my—" Beanie began. But she quickly realized that by defending herself she would only feel worse, less valued, less accepted. She turned away and headed for the swings.

Moments later Charles joined her. "So. The Snob Squad doesn't want you?" he asked.

"Nope. And you want to know why? Partly because I hang out with you!" she lashed out, eager to blame Charles for her popularity problem.

"Ouch. No fair getting nasty *before* you join them, Beanie. Wait till after."

"Don't call me Beanie or Beanbag or anything like that anymore. Call me Beatrice from now on."

Charles looked at her. "Beatrice? No. Sorry. I don't think so."

"Don't think so, what?" Ernestine burst onto the scene, flopping stomach down onto an empty swing.

"Nothing, Ernestine!" said Beanie. "Stop butting in."

"But, but, but. Get it?" Ernestine asked. "I'm butting in. Get it?"

"I really and truly hate school," Beanie said bitterly. "Can't you guys just leave me alone?"

And she wandered away from the other kids toward the edge of the woods. She sat down on the ground, mournfully picking up twigs and snapping them in half while she waited for the bell.

Jerm and Beanie hurried off the bus. Bursting through their back door at three-thirty, together they yelled out, "Mom, we're home."

Beanie dropped her backpack, now full of textbooks, in the middle of the kitchen floor. Jerm did the same.

"Hi!" Mrs. Kingsley said as she entered the kitchen, smiling. "Look at me, fellas. I'm dressed all in black. I'm in mourning."

She opened a black shawl she had spread over her shoulders and spun in a circle like a fashion model. She also wore black jeans and a black hat.

"What for?" asked Jerm.

"I'm mourning the end of our summer vacation."

"I thought moms were supposed to celebrate the first day of school," Beanie said.

"Not me. Check out this black hat I got at Goodwill. Isn't it elegant with this crumpled pink rose stuck on the side?"

"Yeah. Very Squidleyish. Mom, you know what? I bet you're the only mother in the whole of Weymouth who didn't ask her kids how school went today."

"Is that what you want? You guys want me to grill you about school? I can, you know. Or I could consult my magic onion." And she grabbed one from the counter.

"No!" Beanie cried. "Please, don't! If you must know, it was awful!"

"I hate school, Mom. You want to know why?" Jerm said.

"Oh, no," groaned Beanie.

"There are more girls than boys in my class. It's so gross. And you should see this one girl. She's a giant, Mom, I swear. She's abnormal. Totally."

"Jerm, be quiet for a minute. Mom, how was work? What happened?"

"I was there for three hours, from nine till twelve. Everyone was understanding and nice, but there is so much to be done. Details, information to look up and put in order for the cases. I need to constantly double-check my work for mistakes. I was so tired! But I'll get the hang of it again. Don't worry, Beanie."

"Oh, I wasn't worried. But aren't you supposed to stay until three? Didn't you work six hours before?"

"Yes, but I think I should gradually work up to that. Listen, Beanie. Do you think you can cook dinner for us?"

Homework? Dinner? Covering books? When would she get to the hammock and her daydreams? School destroyed your life.

"Yeah," she muttered. "Sure." She picked up her backpack and headed upstairs.

In her room, Beanie lay on the bed, pressing her hot cheek against the smoothness of the pillow, thinking over what had happened that day. She wouldn't cover her textbooks now or read Chapter 1 of her social studies book. That could wait.

Because the sun had beat down on the roof of their small Cape all day, her bedroom was suffocatingly hot under the low upstairs ceiling. Longing for some fresh air, Beanie jumped up and bounded down the stairs and out the front door. She tore across the lawn, heading for the trees in their backyard, and launched herself stomach first, crosswise, into the hammock, setting it swinging.

Ahhh. That was better.

Swinging felt so good. The sensation of weightlessness made Beanie think of kites and birds and flying through the air.

Under the trees, there was always a cool breeze from the bay, especially on September afternoons. Beanie rolled over on her back as the hammock rocked, and wished it could always be summer.

9

"Boo!"

"Aaaah!" Beanie sat straight up, her heart racing. Charles Sprague was grinning down at her. He was wearing his back brace.

"I scared you, didn't I?" Charles said. "Hee, hee."

His scruffy blond hair stuck straight up in uneven spikes because he never combed it. Charles was absolutely not scary. Messy maybe, but not scary. And yet Beanie had been terrified.

"No, Mr. Car Seat, you did not." She was annoyed with him. She hated being scared. She hated not knowing what would happen next. Why couldn't anyone understand that?

"Yes, I did. And don't call me that."

"Fine. But you keep calling me Beanie, and I told you not to. Anyway, don't scare me ever again. I hate it! I hate being scared!" she yelled.

"Jeezum. Calm down, will ya?"

"Okay, sorry," she said. Beanie felt guilty for shouting at him. "You scared me to death. Happy now?"

"I guess. Want to see something weird?" he said cheerfully.

"No. Well, maybe. Where is it, though, 'cause I don't want to get out of the hammock. I'm staying here for the rest of my life."

"You have to come over to my house to see it."

"Nah. I don't want to. Just tell me."

"Nope."

"Come on, Charles."

"Oh, all right. It's the latest X rays of my spine. The curved part is gross. My spine looks like a great big S, and I'm just starting to go into my growth spurt."

"Are you? You think I'm going into a growth spurt, too?" Beanie asked, suddenly curious.

"I don't know. That's not the point. The point is first of all, I might become a radiologist, and second, I'm deformed."

"No you're not, Charles. You shouldn't say that."

"Why not? It's true. My spine is deformed. I bet I'll look like the Hunchback of Notre Dame when I grow up."

"Who?"

"Some bell-ringer guy in an old monster movie," Charles said glumly.

"Charles, you look okay. Really. Your parents are kind of whacked, that's all. That's your only real problem."

"I'm deformed, Beanie. And speaking of problems,

you know what your problem is? You never feel sorry for people. All you care about is yourself."

"That's not true," Beanie said. "I just think that you're going to be okay. I mean, I throw up when I eat chocolate. And Jerm gets strep throat practically every other month. Nobody's perfect."

"This is a deformity and not strep throat, which goes away!" Charles was now yelling at the top of his lungs, just the way his parents did out in the driveway.

"Okay. I heard you! I'm sorry your spine is in an S shape."

"Yeah. So you want to see the X rays?"

"Sure. Bring 'em over," Beanie said.

"I can't. I'm not allowed to take them out of the house."

"Boy. Your mom thinks up more rules . . ."

Charles sighed. "Yeah. Tell me about it."

Charles's mother was a weird mix of strict and casual. The house was a total mess inside. Books were piled up everywhere. Mr. Turtley Wurtley, who Charles's dad claimed was twenty years old, had the run of the house and ate whatever he wanted, not just lettuce but everything, even chocolate ice cream. And Charles never had a bedtime. He could stay up until he felt tired, which was how he had gotten interested in old movies, because they were on late-night TV.

"Hey, what if Mr. Turtley Wurtley had scoliosis? Let's make him a little back brace to wear."

Charles giggled at the thought. "He already has one. His shell."

Beanie grinned, too, and suddenly remembered how much fun it was to hang out with Charles, much more fun than struggling to get into the Snob Squad.

"How come you had to get new X rays, anyway?" she asked.

"Because I've been having more pain in my back. The doctor wants me to wear my brace to school now, at least through this year."

"You're kidding. Wow. Well, then you probably should. That is definitely what you should do."

"Give me a break, Beans. I don't want to, obviously," Charles said. "Can you imagine how much kids would tease me?"

Beanie sighed. "Yeah, I can. But wearing the brace more would help you. And you know what I think would help *me*? Being best, best, best friends with Miranda. How come Barbie and Miranda don't like me? I bet it's because I hang around with you and Jerm."

"You already told me that. Thanks for reminding me, Beanie."

Beanie frowned. It had to be because of Jerm and Charles that the girls didn't like her. Otherwise their rejection meant that there was something wrong with her. "Charles, tell me the truth. Is there anything you don't like about me?"

"No. I like you a lot."

Beanie blushed, feeling guilty that she was ready to ditch Charles to impress Barbie's clique.

"Besides, who cares what those guys think?" Charles said.

"I do! My life stinks, Charles. I need a lot of friends, cool friends," Beanie said.

"Oh, yeah? And what am I? A geek? Let me have a turn in the hammock now. You've had it forever."

"You're not getting a turn. No way."

Charles grabbed the ropes along the edge and slowed the hammock to a stop. "Come on, Beanie. Out!"

"No. Car Seat, cut it out!" Beanie yelled.

"Don't call me that," Charles said, shaking the hammock and trying to tip Beanie out of it.

She held on tight with both hands. "Why not? Don't you ever look at yourself in the mirror?"

Charles dropped the side of the hammock. He pressed his lips together in a thin line. "You need to apologize for that," he said.

"Why?" Beanie asked. "Quit acting so special. Just get over it."

"You're awful, you know that? You *do* belong with those snobby kids like Miranda. I bet you're ashamed of being seen with me."

"No," she mumbled. "That's not true."

But it was true. They both knew that. Beanie was beginning to feel truly awful about what she had said. She knew perfectly well that he'd asked her a hundred times not to call him Car Seat, and he had just finished telling her that his back hurt. But she couldn't retreat. It was best to let Charles know what lengths she was prepared to go to in order to get Barbie and Miranda to accept her into their group. "Well, I guess sometimes I am a little embarrassed," she said slowly.

Charles stared at her. His face turned red and his eyes filled with tears. "You know what? You're as bad as they are. I hope they do let you join."

He turned around and went home.

Beanie lay in the hammock, crying a little and watching the leaves toss overhead. She thought that maybe—except for when she was raging mad at Jerm now and then—it was the first time she had ever intentionally hurt another person. And now that she'd done that, she had a hollow place inside, a place that she was afraid of.

She tipped herself out of the hammock and wandered up the road through the woods, swinging a stick, which made a whooshing sound as she whipped it through the air. She had hurt her very best friend, and he had gone away, maybe forever. And if Barbie and Miranda didn't let her join the Snob Squad, she would have no friends at all from fifth grade probably until college, whenever that was.

There was a trail on the left that started out along the banks of a narrow little brook. It led to a small frog pond where she and Charles had caught tadpoles in glass jars in the spring. Last year, they had built a hideout there of overlapping branches so they could watch the bullfrogs without being seen themselves.

Beanie reached the little pond and their hideout. She crawled inside and sat cross-legged, waiting for the frogs to come out of their hiding places underwater, under logs, or in the mud.

A big spotted bullfrog leaped from under a fallen log right in front of the branch hut. His throat suddenly puffed out like a bubble blown from yellow bubble gum. He looked funny, and Beanie smiled. Other frogs appeared and began their chug-a-rumming, rubber-band-boinging sound. Charles did a great bullfrog imitation.

Beanie felt bad about what she'd said. But she was so angry at everybody that she couldn't imagine herself apologizing. How was she supposed to get used to a sick mom no doctor could help? The only thing she could do to change her life for the better was to somehow make herself extra-perfect. Healthy. Athletic. Rich. Then, even if she wasn't admitted to the Snob Squad, Mrs. Adams might be interested in sort of adopting her. She'd have loads of friends and forget about how worried she was.

She had to drive Charles away, that was all. Beanie knew it was wrong, but not compared to what Miranda had done. She'd shoplifted some earrings in order to stay friends with Barbie. Being intentionally mean to Charles wasn't as bad as stealing, was it? Beanie asked herself. Of course not.

Still, it was a long time before Beanie crawled out of the shelter and went home to start dinner.

10

"Hi, Beanie!" her mother said. "Where on earth have you been?"

"The frog pond."

"You're just in time to help. We're having home-made pizza tonight."

"Pizza again?" Beanie wasn't in the mood.

"Sure. You weren't around, so Jerm decided. Why not?"

"I don't know. No reason."

Her mother hugged her. Beanie pressed her head against her mother's chest, longing to tell her what she had said to Charles, but she knew her mom would be disappointed in her. So she said nothing. And the irritated, mad-at-the-world feeling settled a little deeper inside her and made itself at home.

Jerm had dragged a chair over to the counter. He was busily getting out the measuring cup, a flat pan, and a jar of tomato sauce. Jerm liked helping.

"Why can't we just order a pizza?" Beanie grumbled. "That's what Mrs. Adams does. That's what everybody does."

"Making your own is more fun," her mother said.

"No it's not," Beanie muttered as she washed her hands. "I hate scrubbing the gooey dough out of the bowl afterward."

She wanted to complain about making pizza to prove that it was important to be like kids whose parents bought everything, who ate out at fast-food places every other day, and went skiing, and went to Disney World and summer camp. And had new clothes. Whose moms never bought squashed-up old hats at Goodwill instead of the latest computer games.

"Anyway, you know what? I'm tired of cooking dinner. Miranda never cooks dinner. I bet Charles doesn't, either. I bet I'm the only kid in my class who has to do chores all the time!"

Beanie burst into tears. "And I bet a million billion dollars I'm the only kid in the class with a sick mother!"

"Beanie, sweetheart. Come over here."

Her mother led her to the small sofa and they sat down.

"Jerm, would you please watch TV or look at books in your room for a little while?" Mrs. Kingsley asked. "Now, Beanie, tell me what's going on."

"Nothing. I just don't want to cook dinner every night, that's all."

"Are you worried about my illness?"

"No."

"Oh. I thought maybe you were."

Beanie didn't answer.

While her mother rubbed her back, Beanie gradually calmed down and blew her nose. Then her mother said, "Well, I worry about it sometimes. I worry about my job. Today I was afraid of letting people down. I feel like I can't promise anything to anybody. It's really hard to know what will happen at this point."

Beanie nodded. But what *would* happen to them if her mother couldn't work? Would they starve? She hadn't thought of *that* before. "Can you call Uncle Ozzy? I mean, can you tell him you're not better?"

"Of course, Beanie."

"Do you think he would come help us if you got worse?"

"He might," her mother said slowly. "But, Beanie, there's no way to predict the future based on what's happening today. Today's only one little piece of the puzzle, not the whole shebang. So please don't worry so much. It's not the kind of illness that gets worse and worse. Hey," said her mom. "Come on. I want to show you something I'm making. It's in the basement."

There, downstairs, sitting on the cement floor among the disassembled Haunted House parts were three lawn chairs, completely decorated with weird objects: pink flamingoes jutted from the backs of the chairs, cup holders were duct-taped to the armrests, the seats were draped in purple velvet edged with tiger-striped orange cloth. Plastic toy binoculars hung from cords on the side. Beanie burst out laughing.

"And . . . watch this!" her mother said triumphantly. Mrs. Kingsley plugged in an extension cord and the chairs lit up with little Christmas lights that played "Rudolph, the Red-Nosed Reindeer."

"Musical chairs! Get it?"

"Yeah." Beanie grinned, sitting in one of them. "Cool."

"These, my dear, are the Madame Squidley Musical Lawn Chairs."

"Can I put mine in my room?" Beanie asked.

"Certainly. But keep in mind that they were made for a purpose."

"What's that?"

"We are going to use them for the semiannual driveway/woodpile giant slug hunt."

Beanie laughed. "Is that what the binoculars are for? Tracking slugs?"

"Exactly."

"Wait till I tell Charles. He'll go crazy. Maybe we can make a chair for him, too." Then Beanie remembered that she was trying to get rid of Charles, that he was barely speaking to her, and that there was no way to tell her mother about it.

Her mom sat in one of the chairs.

"Hey, how come you made these today?" Beanie asked. "It wasn't really because of the slugs, right?"

"Actually, because it was my first day back at work, and when I got home, I was feeling sorry for myself. I don't want to be like that. I don't want you to feel sorry for me, either, Beanie. I'm going to fight this thing. If the time comes when we need to get help, okay, then we will. But for now we're going to go on with our lives. Full steam ahead! That's the ticket!"

Get help. There. Her mother had said it. Beanie smiled weakly. "Yeah, I guess."

"Now. Homemade pizza. Come on. After dinner we'll call Uncle Ozzy."

While she was rolling out the yeasty-smelling dough, Beanie kept hearing her mother's words—"if the time comes when we need to get help." From her point of view, the time *had* come. But whom could she find who would listen to her right now? Uncle Ozzy was thousands of miles away. Not across the street. Without Charles, there was nobody she could truly count on.

Later, Beanie sat on the kitchen sofa while her mother dialed Uncle Ozzy's office number in California. Maybe Ozzy wouldn't be in. Maybe the family had gone on vacation, or even moved to Hawaii. "Worrywart," Beanie scolded herself. She had turned herself into such a massive worrier.

Her mother gave her the victory sign. Ozzy had answered the phone.

Beanie listened as her mother explained about her fatigue and fever. That she got quickly exhausted, that she had to rest frequently throughout the day, and that exercise made her weak and faint. She also told Ozzy that every once in a while, all her muscles seemed to turn rigid and jerk, but the doctor explained that it wasn't epilepsy. Then they talked about Ozzy's work and the girls, Lee Ann and Chelsey.

After half an hour, her mother hung up and turned to Beanie. "So. Ozzy will come out at the end of September. He's going to help us plan the next few months, okay, Beanie?"

"Are the girls coming? And Auntie Jane?"

"No, just Ozzy. You can be part of the planning committee, all right?"

⁓

Every morning at 7:20, the school bus stopped at the corner in front of Charles's driveway. Beanie, up and ready early, went outside to wait. Jerm tagged along behind. Still eating his toaster waffle, he followed her out the door, dragging his backpack on the ground. They glanced sideways at each other, then began to run, racing for the first turn in the hammock. Beanie won.

"That's because of my waffle," Jerm said. "That's the only reason you beat me."

Beanie ignored him.

Jerm sat down under the trees, nibbling around the outside edges of his waffle. He glanced at Beanie sadly, his round, wire-rimmed glasses making him look extra-vulnerable. "You know, I would like a turn next," Jerm said in a hurt voice. "And I think I'm being pretty patient."

"Ahhhhh!" Beanie screamed to the treetops. "Spare me!"

"Charles told me you were mean to him and called him names," Jerm said. "You should say you're sorry, Beanie."

"It's none of your business. So stay out of it, dude," Beanie answered.

"Uh-oh. Bus! It's early!" yelled Jerm, scrambling to his feet.

The kids grabbed their backpacks and ran, sneakers pounding, to the corner. Miranda came running from her end of the street.

"Oh, hi, Beanie. Guess what? I'm not taking the bus home today." Miranda panted as she climbed on. "I'm going to the hairdresser's after school. I asked Miss Bennett where she got her hair cut. I'm getting mine cut exactly the same way at the exact same salon."

"You are?" Beanie looked at Miranda's mass of curls.

"Yeah. A shag cut. Then, when it's in layers, I can shape it with a curling iron if I need to. That's what Miss Bennett does."

Beanie stared at Miranda. How had she found these things out about their teacher so quickly? Why did she want to turn into a photocopy of Miss Babysitter Bennett? In fourth grade, Beanie and Miranda had played together. They'd read horse stories out loud to each other. What was going on here?

"Don't you think she's just so incredibly attractive?" Miranda asked. For once Miranda sat down in the same seat Beanie did. Charles got on last and pushed past on his way to the back, not looking at Beanie.

"No," Beanie answered.

"She's so sweet, I think. And Barbie's coming with me," Miranda said. "She's getting a shag cut, too. So we'll be twins."

"Wow. Cool," said Beanie tonelessly, frowning to hide the stab of pain she felt. She sighed.

Maybe, Beanie thought, my problem is that I don't like or care about anybody, just the way Charles said. She quickly pulled *The Wind in the Willows* out of her pack and read about Toad and Badger the rest of the way to school, while Miranda carefully scraped purple nail polish off her fingernails.

11

THURSDAY. ONLY THE SECOND DAY OF FIFTH grade, and Beanie was alone on the playground. In fourth grade, she remembered, she'd had plenty of friends. A big group of girls her age, including Miranda and Barbie, had played together every single day, racing one another for the swings, playing jump rope and kickball, running around, leaping over puddles, sliding on the black ice that formed on the blacktop in winter, always laughing. School had been fun, at least for most of the year.

Now she stood by herself, pushing sand into a little heap with the toe of her sneaker and smoothing it out again, as Miranda and Barbie leaned against the wall by the playground door, talking, waiting for the morning bell. Charles and Ernestine Brown were on the first set of swings near the rhododendron bushes. Beanie was avoiding them.

Beanie knew Miranda and Barbie wanted to be the first ones inside today so they could talk with Miss Bennett about their trip to the hairdresser's. She clenched her fists and wished and wished that they would call her over.

But of course they didn't.

She ran to the farthest set of swings, dropping her pack and beginning to swing as though she didn't have a care in the world. Beanie smiled, remembering the Musical Lawn Chairs, her mom's secret weapon against self-pity.

But wait. Had Beanie been feeling sorry for herself? She slowed her swing to a stop and thought for a moment. Yes. Pretty much all the time since her mom's doctor's appointment, ever since Madame Olivia's fortune-telling. Angry and sorry for herself, both, and it was making her feel rotten inside. It made the center of her chest tight. It filled her up with a sticky, gloppy goop like black oatmeal with Elmer's glue mixed in so that nothing else could get in or out.

Was her misery because she was stuck on her daydreams? On replacing her mother with someone perfect, on imagining that she, Beanie, was stylish and mature, on trying to wish away Charles, Jerm, and Ernestine? Had she gone completely nuts? She needed to talk to Charles.

But Weymouth Elementary School didn't allow kids much privacy or time for thinking, and now here came buttinsky Ernestine, moving over from the other end of the swings.

"Hi!" Ernestine said.

Beanie didn't answer. But then she felt mad at

herself for being unfriendly. Daydream Beanie acted that way, the one who didn't share and who drifted in the hammock. Stop it, Beanie told herself. Stop it. Stop it.

"What's up?" Ernestine asked.

"Nothing. I'm a swing-a-holic!" she yelled, pretending to be cheerful.

"Yeah? So?" Ernestine popped a huge pink bubble of gum. "Ask me if I'm impressed. Hey, how's your teacher this year?"

"Miss Bennett? I don't know. I hate her. I think she's ugly."

Beanie pulled forward, straining her toes, her grip. Up to the sky, she thought. Up to the sky.

"I have Woodward. He's gonna work our butts off," Ernestine said. "He said 'butts,' too. In class. I told my mom when I got home."

Pop went the gum, sticking to Ernestine's nose. She carefully peeled off the film of gum and pushed it back into her mouth. She smacked loudly when she chewed. Year round, she wore huge, baggy mohair sweaters that her mom knit for her. Her nose ran a lot, and she pushed it up to scratch, rubbing it with the back of her hand all the time until there was a red crease across the bridge.

"He said we're getting forty minutes of homework every night. But I don't care. I'm not doing any homework. My parents won't make me, either. Hey, your snooty friend Miranda is going inside, and the bell didn't even ring. What's that all about?"

"I don't know."

It could be dangerous to give Ernestine too much information. Although she talked a lot, she wasn't particularly friendly or loyal and would turn on you in an instant.

"Are you taking an instrument?" Ernestine asked.

"You mean a band instrument?"

"Yeah. Take trumpet. I am. That way I can annoy the whole house. Or I might take drums, but I heard you have to practice on a rubber pad, so what's the point? Not that I'm going to practice or anything. Didn't Miss Bennett tell you about instrumental music yesterday? We get out of class for it. That's why I'm doing it. And if it's a hard instrument, or you really stink at it, who knows, you might get out twice a week. There's a hard instrument called bassoon. You should take that."

"Yeah? Bassoon?" Beanie's ears perked up.

"My mom says it's the hardest instrument."

Now, here was something to be explored. She could escape class to play bassoon? This was news. Maybe Miranda would think she was fun to be with if she played the bassoon.

"Come on. There's the bell." Ernestine dragged her feet in the sand to stop the swing.

Beanie leaped off her swing, even though it wasn't allowed, pretending for a moment to be an Olympic long jumper. "Fifty-six feet eight inches," she said. She raised her arms in the air, listening to imaginary applause. "Thank you. Thank you."

"What are you doing?" Ernestine asked, rubbing her nose.

"I was jumping for Poland."

"What?"

"In the Olympics."

"Poland?"

"Never mind."

Charles would have understood at once, Beanie thought. She looked around for him. There he was, dragging his backpack across the blacktop to the lines that were forming.

With a pang, Beanie wondered if the heavy pack full of books hurt his back. It must. Gosh, how could she never have thought of that before? She could have offered to carry a few of his books for him. Maybe he was right. Maybe all she did was think about herself and her problems. Maybe she was a self-pitying slug, slithering along on her narrow trail of slime.

"Are you deaf?" Ernestine said in her face. "I said 'Come on.' "

Ernestine and Beanie crossed the playground and were the last to get in line right behind Charles. Now they had to stand there, waiting for two hundred kids to enter the school in single file—quietly—through the double doors. Barbie and Miranda were outside again. Could they have been thrown out for being inside before the bell? They now had the first two spots in line.

Ernestine yawned loudly. She sniffled and rubbed her nose, then sat down on the ground.

"Sit down. Take a load off," she advised Beanie.

Beanie obligingly sat on her pack.

"Hope your sandwich isn't in there," Charles said.

He was talking to her again! Beanie felt a burst of happiness like the white brilliance of a flashbulb from a camera. Her old pal, Charles Sprague!

"Oh, no!" Beanie wailed cheerfully. "My peach!"

She stood up and unzipped the outside pocket. A fresh peach had squished all over the inside. Beanie pulled it out by the slimy pit and held it with her thumb and pointer finger, not sure what to do with it. She was afraid to hurl it into the bushes by the door. So she stood there, holding it. Peach juice trickled down her wrist and onto her sleeve.

"Yuck!"

"God, Beanie. Don't be such a spaz about everything. Why don't you just eat it?" Ernestine said.

"Yeah? Okay."

Beanie scooped out the inside of the pocket and bit into what was left of the peach.

"That's unsanitary, eating like that," Charles said. "Your fingers are covered with tiny germs, carrying awful diseases. Like mad cow disease. Or hoof and mouth or . . ." He seemed happy to be talking to her, too.

"Peaches don't carry mad cow disease, for your information. And fingers? Who cares about finger germs? What about the inside of that backpack? Did you think of that?" Ernestine said.

"Charles is going to be a doctor," Beanie explained.

"Yeah. And fingers are the most disgusting part—" Charles began.

"I said *quiet*!" roared an adult voice.

Mr. Woodward stood by the door, glaring at them. Beanie jumped as she finally realized that Mr. Woodward had been talking to her and that all two hundred fourth and fifth graders were silent, heads turned, looking at the three kids at the end of the line.

"You three in the back. Up here. By me. *Now*!" bellowed Mr. Woodward.

"Uh-oh," muttered Ernestine. "I bet we get detention."

Beanie's cheeks burned with embarrassment. Glumly she picked up her backpack, wiped her sticky fingers on her jeans, and followed the other two up front while the rest of the kids watched.

"Against the wall," said Mr. Woodward.

Beanie dropped her bag at her feet and leaned against the bricks, ducking her head so she wouldn't catch anyone's eye.

She heard Barbie whisper to Miranda, "Ernestine's hair is the pits."

"Yeah, but all she needs is a good haircut. Listen to what Beanie did at my house during a sleepover. She is such a baby. In the middle of the night, she left. She had to go home!" Miranda replied.

Beanie stared at Miranda in dismay. How could Miranda have said that? It was private. She hadn't told a soul that Miranda had shoplifted the earrings. She'd kept her promise.

Now Miranda was giggling with a hand over her mouth as she and Barbie led the line inside. "See ya, Beanie Baby," Miranda whispered sarcastically as she disappeared into the shadowy hallway.

"Beanie Baby. That's a good one," Barbie said. "Hey, you want to sleep over this weekend, Miranda? You can, as long as you don't have to go home in the middle of the night."

Beanie stared after them as they went inside. They were mean. And here she was, desperately kissing up to mean kids. Charles had told her that fifty times before, but it hadn't sunk in till now. And Charles didn't even know they shoplifted candy and earrings.

Mr. Woodward pointed at Charles, Beanie, and Ernestine with his pen. "Listen up, you three. Just a warning today. But you better be on your best behavior tomorrow morning. Got it?"

Charles and Beanie nodded. But Ernestine said, "Mr. Woodward, is the bassoon a hard instrument?"

"Inside, Miss Brown."

12

AT LUNCH, MIRANDA AND BARBIE QUICKLY PICKED out a table where other members of the Snob Squad could join them. The group of girls shrieked and giggled so loudly that the lunch ladies came by twice to tell them to quiet down.

Robbers, shoplifters, thought Beanie, glancing at their table. I hope the mall police catch them. That would be funny. But wait—how could they be so popular? They *stole* things. How could she be friends with such creepy kids? She'd insulted Charles just to try to impress them? She knew her mom would be shocked about the stealing. Feeling guilty and awkward, Beanie struggled to eat her lunch.

Charles and Ernestine sat with Beanie. No one else came near them. They argued about Mr. Woodward's threat.

"He can't give us detention. All I did was ask if playing the bassoon was hard," Ernestine said.

"So? He can make us stay after," Charles said. "Any teacher can do that."

"But I didn't do anything! You guys were the noisy ones."

"We were lucky he just gave us a warning, Ernestine. Teachers can put behavior problems on your school record, you know. And I want to go to medical school. I can't have bad stuff on my record," Charles said.

"Give me a break, Charles," Ernestine argued. "Have you seen these detention slips? You can get check marks for swearing or hitting, things like that. Not for asking what a bassoon is. Not for talking during recess."

"Recess was over," Charles said. "Don't change facts, Ernestine."

"I'm going to play the bassoon," said Beanie dreamily.

Ernestine snorted. "Yeah. You've never even heard one."

"Neither have you," Beanie said lamely.

"That's dumb. Of course I have. You know my mother is harpist for the Portland Symphony. I've heard tons of bassoons."

"Tons?" asked Charles. He methodically peeled his orange. "Tons of bassoons? Not possible."

"Your mother raises sheep, I thought," Beanie said.

"She gets credit for the sheep, but I have to do most of the work so she won't hurt her fingers for harp practice. Well, I do some of the work. My dad helps. Mother dyes and weaves the wool. And knits, too.

Anyway, you guys have to go sign up for band instruments. I get to take my trumpet home today."

Charles rolled his eyes.

"Yeah, Charles? What instrument are you going to take, then?" Ernestine asked.

"I don't know. Probably drums."

"Hey," Ernestine said, "let's go to the band room now so you guys can sign up."

"And leave the lunchroom?" Beanie asked. "We can't."

"Sure we can. We're not little kids. This is fifth grade, Beanie. I walk around the halls all the time. If someone asks us where we're going, just say we have an appointment with Mr. Flagg. Come on."

They walked straight out of the lunchroom and down the hall without a problem.

"Hi, Mr. Flagg," Ernestine called out as they entered the band room.

The music teacher was a slight man. He nearly always wore corduroy sports jackets and chinos. He had combed a few strands of hair sideways across his bald spot. "Hello, Ernestine," he answered. "Hello, friends of Ernestine. Beatrice. Charles."

"Hi. I'd like to sign up for bassoon," Beanie said.

"Well, Beatrice, I wish that were possible, but I don't usually let fifth graders start on an instrument like that. Bassoons are frightfully expensive, for one thing, and the holes are very far apart. It's hard for young fingers to spread that far."

"But I could do it. I know I could," Beanie protested. "I could work extra hard. I could come in for extra practice." She had already worked out a daydream in which she had a bassoon solo at the annual Christmas concert. She was wearing a green velvet dress and . . . Oh. Mr. Flagg was talking again.

"What we really need in the band is clarinets. You could start on clarinet, get used to the reed, playing music, and so on, and then in seventh grade you could switch to bassoon."

"Seventh grade?" Beanie asked.

It seemed light-years away. Mr. Flagg went into the instrument closet and came out with a black leather case.

"Now, Beatrice, you'll have to buy the reeds on your own. Start with a one and a half, but buy some number twos also. And get some cork grease. You're going to need cork grease. Let me just copy down the ID number from that clarinet. Here's your permission slip. As soon as I get that back, you can take home a clarinet."

He handed Beanie the slip. "Congratulations," he added.

"Thank you," she said wanly.

"Can you put me down for drums?" Charles asked.

"Certainly. You'll need your own set of sticks and a practice pad for home."

Back out in the hall, Ernestine said, "Beanie, you didn't even stick up for yourself. You waffled. You should have picked the tuba or some other weird instrument when he said no to the bassoon."

"And you're going to need cork grease. Buy a lot of it," Charles said to her. "I wonder how that would look in my hair."

As they trailed slowly down the hall toward the playground for after-lunch recess, with Beanie bringing up the rear, they rounded a corner and ran smack into Miss Bennett.

"Excuse me, people, but what are you doing inside?" Miss Bennett asked. "It's recess."

"Oh, we had to go to the band room to sign up for instruments," Ernestine said smoothly.

Beanie's heart sank. In trouble again. First she had to tag along with Charles and Ernestine, and then she had to get a warning from Mr. Woodward, and then she had to sign up for an instrument she didn't want. Now she found herself glaring at her teacher.

"Excuse me, young lady," Miss Bennett said angrily. "What is that expression for?"

"Huh?" Beanie asked. "What expression?"

"You two head on outside," Miss Bennett said to Ernestine and Charles. "Beanie, into the classroom. I'll be in to talk with you in a minute."

"But I didn't do . . ." Beanie began, but Miss Bennett was already striding down the hallway toward the principal's office. "Anything," Beanie added softly.

"Not your lucky day, Beanbag," Ernestine said. "Toodles."

Toodles? Beanie wanted to sock Ernestine.

Instead, she trailed into the empty classroom like a wilted violet and sat down at her desk. She laid her head down on her folded arms. Did everyone in the world hate her by now? The whole year was ruined, probably. Her mom was sick with an incurable disease. Her dream family hadn't come for her. There wasn't going to be a limousine. Mrs. Adams knew her family needed help, and she had even said, "Maybe we can . . ." But now Beanie knew that Mrs. Adams would never make time to help her. Mrs. Adams already had a family, and Beanie realized that the Adamses had their own problems.

Her future was sadly foggy, and Miranda and Barbie were going for haircuts. The bassoon was out of the question. Her jeans were worn out. And Charles was probably still mad at her.

Now she decided that she hated Miss Bennett. Already Beanie could tell she was the kind who played favorites among the kids. And she knew she wasn't going to be a favorite. Clearly Miss Bennett had picked only on her, excusing Ernestine and Charles. Ernestine was the one who should have been punished, for this morning, as well.

Everyone else was outside now, having fun. Playing, laughing. Tears trickled down her cheeks.

Miss Bennett touched her shoulder. "Beanie? Are you all right?" she asked.

Beanie looked up at her teacher's blue eyes, rimmed with shiny, sparkly gold eye shadow. She looked perfect, just like a model in a magazine photo, while Beanie's mom had to walk very slowly most of the time and often had a fever. It wasn't fair. Beanie could smell Miss Bennett's perfume, a heavy, sweet floral scent.

"I hate you," Beanie said without realizing what she had been going to say until it hung there, in the air. Spoken aloud and no way to take it back. What had she done?

Miss Bennett's eyes narrowed. "I don't like your attitude, young lady. You will miss the bus today. The office will call your mother and have her come pick you up at three-thirty. Now, head down. And stay that way until the other kids come in from recess."

Miss Bennett swept from the room, taking her perfumy smell with her. Beanie sat there, her head cradled in her arms. She wished she could melt into a puddle of invisible ink and sink down through the floor and disappear without even leaving a spot. No one would know what had happened to her. She wanted to be nothing, nowhere, forever.

13

A LITTLE AFTER THREE-THIRTY, BEANIE CLIMBED into the front seat of her mother's car and shut the door, while her mother and Miss Bennett stood by the entrance to the school, talking. Beanie stared miserably at her shoes.

Jerm leaned forward. "What happened, Beanie?" he asked. "What did you do? How come you weren't on the bus?"

"I didn't do anything. It was that idiot, Ernestine."

"Ernestine Brown? Come on, Beanie. Tell me. Please?"

"No! Leave me alone."

Then her mother said goodbye to Miss Bennett, walked slowly to the driver's side of the car, and got in.

"Ready to go, my dear?" she asked.

Beanie nodded.

"Hey, I brought you an apple. I thought you might be hungry. Here."

Beanie took the new fall apple and bit into it. It tasted fresh and tangy, not at all like a school lunch apple, much better than the bits of smushed peach she had scooped out of her backpack.

"What happened to Beanie, Mom? Was she bad?" Jerm asked.

"It's really not something I want to talk to you about," their mother said. "It's something private."

Beanie relaxed a little. She appreciated that her mother wouldn't talk about what had happened with snoopy Jeremiah eavesdropping in the backseat.

"I heard Miss Bennett is a really mean teacher," Jerm said.

"You did not!" Beanie exclaimed. "Stop making things up!"

"Guys. I'm going to ask for ten minutes of silence."

"Next one to speak is a monkey for a week," Jerm whispered, just to see what would happen.

"Jerm!" Mrs. Kingsley said in a very stern voice. He sat back in his seat.

Sometimes her mother did this if she sensed a squabble was brewing. Right now, ten minutes would get them all the way home and at least partway into the house. That was good. And then maybe her mother would forget about the little incident today with Miss Bennett.

"When we get home, Beanie, I'd like you to go up to your room. I'll meet you there."

Her mother wouldn't forget. Beanie sighed. She didn't know what she would say, except that she felt awful about everything. Even about her mom having to come pick her up.

Mostly she wondered why things were happening the way they were, which was not the way she wanted. Why wasn't she able to control her life even a tiny bit? And so, feeling awful in general, she started to cry, but very quietly, keeping her face turned toward the window so her mother and Jerm couldn't see.

In her room, Beanie grabbed her Kleenex box and flopped onto her bed with it. She pulled off her shoes and socks and tossed them on the floor so she wouldn't get her almost-new quilt dirty. She traced her finger along the edges of the soft pastel colors. They had bought the quilt last winter, when her mom had had more energy. Before that awful April when they both got sick. Beanie had gotten better, so why hadn't her mom? She couldn't figure that out. Was the doctor right when he said maybe nothing was wrong with her? Was her mom crazy?

Beanie pressed her palms over her eyes so hard she saw flashes of white light. No. She wouldn't think about that. Her mom was not crazy. That would be the worst, scariest thing of all to think about.

Her bedroom door opened.

"Hi," her mother said in a serious voice.

"Hi," Beanie replied.

Her mother crossed the room and sat beside her on the bed. "Beanie, I'm shocked by what Miss Bennett told me. She said you told her that you hated her. Is that right?"

"Yes."

"You've never said anything like that before in your life, that I know of. Can you tell me why you feel that way? Did she do something to you?"

Beanie shook her head, starting to cry again. How could she tell her mother all the worries she had? When her mom tried to reassure her, she only felt worse.

"It's Miranda's fault," she said finally through her tears.

"What's her fault?"

"I didn't want to be friends with Ernestine this year. Because she follows me everywhere and talks non-stop. She's the one who said we had to go to the band room at lunchtime. And before school she got me and Charles in trouble, too. I wanted to be friends with Miranda, but she . . . I guess she doesn't like me."

"She's not very aware of others, is she?" Mrs. Kingsley said.

"No," Beanie replied. "Plus she's spoiled."

"Okay, but, Beanie, I still don't understand. Why did you say you hated Miss Bennett?"

"I don't know. It just sort of flew out of my mouth. I didn't mean to. I don't know why I did it. I hate Mrs. Adams, too. Because . . . because . . . she said she would talk to me, but she never did. And they're healthy and you're not. And it's not fair." Beanie began to sob.

Her mom hugged her tightly. "Oh, sweetie. I'm

sorry. Life isn't always particularly fair. But I'm not so very sick, we have to remember that."

"You're sick enough," Beanie mumbled.

"Yes."

Finally her mother said, "You know you can't talk to teachers that way, right?"

Beanie nodded.

"And you won't ever, ever do that again?"

"No," Beanie said, then added in a shaky voice, "But, Mom, one thing is—she plays favorites."

Mrs. Kingsley sighed. "Some teachers do that. They shouldn't, but they do."

"I guess."

Beanie wanted to ask more about this, but she could see that her mother looked unusually tired. Normally her mom would have been resting from three to four, but today she'd had to wait for Jerm to get off the bus, then drive to the school to pick up Beanie.

Beanie's thoughts leapfrogged: she remembered Charles dragging his heavy backpack across the playground. "I might help Charles carry his books 'cause his back hurts," she said.

"That's a good idea."

"But, Mom, Miranda doesn't like me. She only likes Barbie."

"Of course she likes you, Beanie."

"Not anymore."

"Well, she's making a big mistake. I like you!" her mother said, giving her a big hug. "I love you!"

Beanie smiled. "That's not the same thing," she said.

"It may not be the same, but right now it'll have to do. So, listen, you put your life in order here, and come on downstairs when you're ready, okay?" Her mother gave her one more squeeze.

"Okay," Beanie said.

"Mom! *Mom*!" Jerm roared from his room. "Yoohoo! You can't spend all afternoon talking to Beanie. I have problems in school, too. I'm not adjusting well to my all-day schedule."

"Oh, Lord," Mrs. Kingsley muttered.

"First grade isn't easy for anybody, you know," he bellowed.

In spite of herself, Beanie burst out laughing.

"Oh, by the way, we *are* going hiking this weekend," her mom said.

"We are? Really? Where?" Beanie asked.

"Tumbledown Mountain. And we'll camp overnight at Loon Lake."

"Loon Lake?" Beanie was confused. Was it really okay for her mother to go hiking when she'd had trouble playing four square? What would Dr. Howell say?

"Yup. I thought it would be good for us to get out of the house and do something fun, something we enjoyed doing together. Last weekend I was afraid. But now that I'm back at work and not finding that too hard, I think I can do it. The doctor sees no reason not to resume normal activities, so let's go!"

"Cool. Hey, Mom?"

"Yeah?"

"Could you not tell Jerm about what happened today?"

"Sure thing."

"Oh. And here's my permission slip so I can take clarinet for band." Beanie dug into her pocket and handed her mother a badly crumpled sheet of paper.

"Okay. Anything else?"

"I need some reeds and cork grease," Beanie said in a small voice. "And I have a few more papers. I'll show them to you later."

Her mother closed the door gently behind her.

After dinner, and after the six-thirty news, Beanie, her mother, and Jerm were all sitting on the living room couch. Her mom had just finished reading *Yertle the Turtle* by Dr. Seuss to Jerm, and Beanie was handing her mom different official school notices that had to be signed. Suddenly her mother mispronounced a word. "So band practice is on . . . buh-errrrmm-bbssss. Buhnnuhh." She stopped speaking.

The kids glanced sharply at her.

"Mom?" Beanie asked in a small voice. "Are you okay?"

"Uhhh . . ." She shook her head. "Nnnuhh. Cuh-cuh . . ." Her arms flew up, and she blinked rapidly and hard. Her head jerked backward.

"Jerm, move!" Beanie cried. "Mom! Lie down!"

Beanie yanked Jerm out of the way. "Go get a cold washcloth, Jerm. Quick!"

Her mother lay down, and abruptly her legs stiffened, her teeth clenched, and her back arched rigidly.

"Are you breathing? Mom? Are you okay?" Beanie grabbed her hand, terrified.

Her mom nodded stiffly and looked into Beanie's eyes to show she could hear, that she understood. Jerm ran in with the washcloth, and Beanie laid it across her mother's neck. Mrs. Kingsley's whole body jerked a few more times, but she seemed to be breathing more easily now. Beanie and Jerm stood without moving, staring at her.

"Thanks, guys," she said finally in a choked voice.

Beanie sank to the floor in relief. The paroxysm was over. For now. But what if it happened again? What if it happened on Tumbledown Mountain?

On Friday, Miss Bennett had 10:30 playground duty. Barbie, Miranda, and the other Snob Squad girls stood clustered around her, admiring her hair and clothes. All the boys except Charles were playing touch football, using a rolled-up old ski hat as a ball. Charles finally wandered over to the swings and sat beside Beanie.

"What's up?" he asked.

"Huh? Nothing."

"Why didn't you tell me you're sorry yet?" he asked.

"Sorry?" She shrugged. "I just didn't."

"Beanie, something's happened to you. You're always in such a bad mood."

"I am not."

"Yes you are. I bet you're in puberty."

"I am not. Shut up, Charles. Anyway, if I am, why aren't you in a bad mood, too?"

"Me?" Charles stared at her. "Boy, are you crazy or what? Why would I be in a bad mood?"

"Because your spine is messed up. And you have to wear a car seat thing on your back. You're deformed, Charles Car Seat Sprague. You said so yourself!" Beanie shouted. "Don't you realize your whole life is messed up?"

"My whole life isn't messed up. Only a tiny unimportant part of it is. You know what? I thought we could be friends again, at least sometimes. But I guess not."

He got up and walked away.

I don't care, Beanie thought as she watched him leave. "I don't care! I don't care!" she yelled after him. "You know why? Because I might have to look after my mom."

Charles turned around. Slowly he came back. "What do you mean?"

"Last night, when my mom was going over our school papers—you know, about bringing a lock for a gym locker, and the thing about instrumental music—her voice stopped working. She stopped speaking. When she tried to talk again, only a muddled-up noise came out instead of words. And then her body began to jerk. And her muscles went rigid. Then it stopped, and she lay on the sofa, looking completely exhausted. It was so scary."

"Wow," Charles said.

"What if one day my mother can't talk ever again? What if she has to use a cane? And maybe even a wheelchair like that horrible creepy lady in the Haunted House? And I'll have to cook dinner—for the rest of my life!" Beanie's nose and eyes stung as she squashed her sobs deep inside.

"This is terrible. Beanie, you need to get help," Charles said.

"My uncle is coming from San Francisco in a few weeks. I'm hoping we can get a cleaning lady."

"But what about nights? She seems to do worse later in the day."

Beanie nodded. "I'm calling Dr. Howell again," she decided. "We're going to Tumbledown, after all. I'll ask him about nights and the camping trip, too."

When the recess bell rang, Beanie walked indoors and sat at her desk. She took out her spelling workbook and opened it to the right page and smoothed it neatly. She would behave herself and work hard. She would pay attention to Lesson Two. Homonyms. Yes. Very important.

Beanie did five of them before losing interest. She laid her head down. She didn't care one fig about homonyms. Hair. Hare. Those were homonyms. Big deal.

Pair. Fill in the blank. Beanie yawned a huge yawn. Ho hum diddley dum. Pair. What went with that? Pear that you eat. That was it. Pear. Who cared? When her mom had talked, only noises had come out.

⁓

As soon as Beanie got home, she went over to Charles's house and banged on the door.

"Hi," she said sheepishly. "I need to call the doctor, and I don't want Jerm to hear."

"Yeah. All right," Charles said.

They opened the phone book. Beanie dialed Dr. Howell's number and told the secretary it was urgent.

"Yes, young lady." Dr. Howell came on the line far faster than she'd expected. "I had a call from your uncle a few days ago. He made an appointment. Let's see. October first, we all get together."

"Oh. Dr. Howell, my mom is not okay now. Last night was so terrible. We were on the sofa, talking and stuff, and her words came out jumbled up. And then her body jerked very, very hard and got all stiff. We didn't know what to do. But then it stopped."

"And now she's back to normal?" he asked.

"She was very tired out afterward. I guess she's fine now. But we need someone to help us. Do you know someone who can stay with us, like live at our house or something?"

"No, Beatrice. I don't. But that's not a bad idea. Maybe your uncle can help locate someone to live in."

"Yes," said Beanie. "But wait! You know what else? Tomorrow we're going camping."

"Good, good. That sounds like fun," the doctor said.

"Good? What if she starts talking funny there and her body jerks in the woods? What if she gets so tired she can't walk anymore?" Beanie wailed.

"I wouldn't worry too much. Usually, with rest, she manages to recover fairly quickly. So that's what you'll do. Rest. All right? These crisis episodes of hers do pass, so you'll just have to wait for her to recover and go on."

"Okay," Beanie muttered. "You're no better than Madame Olivia."

"Who?" Dr. Howell asked.

"I went to a fortune-teller named Madame Olivia. She said I had a foggy future."

Dr. Howell laughed. Then he said, "I have to go now, Beatrice."

"My nickname is Beanie."

"Goodbye, then, Beanie. Have a good trip."

"Goodbye."

"Well?" asked Charles.

"Well, nothing. He seems nice, but he doesn't really suggest anything. He just says she has to rest. Hey! Want to come camping with us?"

"I can't. I have to wear my back brace all weekend and go to my dad's. My parents are having this completely weird, great big meeting about me."

But Beanie wasn't interested. She was preoccupied

with her own problems. "Dr. Howell says getting live-in help is a good idea. I don't know how to do that. My uncle's coming, but I'm not sure we can wait for him."

"We can ask my mom what to do. Maybe there's a student at the university who could stay with you guys. Let me ask her, okay?"

"Yeah. Sure. Thanks, Charles."

Beanie knew that underneath he was still angry with her, but for some reason, she just couldn't bring herself to apologize. She clenched her fists, gritted her teeth, and tried, but nothing came out.

"See ya," she finally said and let herself out.

14

AFTER WORK ON FRIDAY, MRS. KINGSLEY RESTED the remainder of the day, saving her energy for the trip. She gave Beanie lists of things to assemble in the kitchen—sleeping bags, matches, flashlights, backpacks. That night, the Kingsleys put their tent, an ice chest full of food, jackets, clothes, trail map, and the rest of their camping gear in the car. They were ready at last to set off for Tumbledown Mountain.

They left the house at 7:00 a.m. on Saturday and headed north for two hours on narrow, poorly paved back roads. Finally they reached the curve in the road that revealed the shimmering surface of Loon Lake, with the mountain a broad massive shape beside it.

"I see it first! I see it first!" Jerm cried. "Loon Toon Lake. Looney Tune Lake. And look! There's Tumbledumbledown Mountain!"

"If there are any loons, you'll scare the daylights out of them with that yelling," Beanie said. Although she now leaned forward against her seat belt, as well.

"Tumbledumble Loon Toon . . ."

"Jeremiah, please, tone it down," their mom said

distractedly. "Your voice is so piercing. This is a lot of driving for me, so please, pipe down."

Beanie turned around in her seat, and she and Jerm glanced at each other. Beanie didn't see how her mom was ever going to make the nearly four-mile hike, anyway. Two miles were uphill climbing that almost never leveled off. The path up Tumbledown was not only moderately steep but also boulder-strewn and crisscrossed by small streams.

Jerm was quiet for a moment, then asked, "Hey, Mom, can we have lunch now? I'm starving."

"Jerm! It's not even nine o'clock, you bozo," Beanie said.

"Mom! She called me a bozo."

"She meant it as a compliment," Mom said. "Bozo was a clown with lovely orange hair."

"And a big red nose," Beanie added.

"It wasn't a compliment. She's trying to hurt my feelings."

"Kids! Stop!" Mrs. Kingsley said, the stress in her voice obvious.

Beanie closed her eyes. Jerm's voice was shrill. She felt tired, too, and dizzy. "I'm getting a migraine," she announced, although she'd never had one in her life.

"Join the club," her mother muttered.

At nine-thirty, they reached the little sandy parking lot at the base of the Tumbledown trail and piled out of the car.

"Now we can have a sandwich, right, Mom?" Jerm asked.

Mrs. Kingsley smiled. "Sure. The peanut butter ones are for snacks. The tuna are for lunch. Or you could just have an apple."

"Sandwich," Jerm decided.

Beanie took one, too, and ate it in the parking area while they unloaded the car. Her mother looked pale, with dark rings under her eyes, but she acted as though nothing were wrong. Both Beanie and Jerm had a small daypack with a windbreaker, hat, two apples, chocolate bar, juice pack, and a whistle in case they got lost.

Beanie turned around and looked out across the parking lot to Loon Lake beyond. It was a wide lake, choppy with small waves from the stiff breeze that blew from the north. The water was a brilliant peacock blue, contrasting with the sprinkling of newly yellowing leaves on the maple trees that lined the shore.

"I wonder if we'll hear a loon," Beanie said to Jerm.

"Maybe when we're falling asleep. Or first thing in the morning. That's when I always hear them. Come on, let's go, you guys. Mom, hurry up."

"Just a minute," Mrs. Kingsley called out, tying her windbreaker around her waist.

"Well, I'm starting," Jerm said. "I'll run ahead and check out the trail for you guys."

"No, Jerm," said Beanie. "We can't do it that way."

"Explorers always do it that way. A scout goes first. See ya," Jerm said.

He bounded off up the path, sending loose pebbles rattling down around Beanie's feet.

"Don't run, goofball. You'll get tired out right at the beginning."

"Slow down, Jerm. I don't want you dashing off like that," Mrs. Kingsley called. But he paid no attention. "Oh, for heaven's sake. Beanie, see if you can't go after him and stop him."

Beanie took off, running at first. Almost at once the path grew steeper, but still Jerm scampered ahead. Beanie clambered after him.

"Jerm! You complete and utter bozo!" she yelled.

"Run, run, fast as you can. Can't catch me, I'm the gingerbread man," she heard as she watched Jerm's turquoise sweatshirt vanish up the trail.

Annoyed, Beanie paused for a moment to catch her breath. Hurrying uphill over tree roots, slippery leaves, piles of acorns, and rocks was hard work. It seemed to be easier for Jerm simply because he was smaller.

"He is such a jerk," she said out loud, then renewed her efforts to overtake him.

Jerm must have grown tired at last, and Beanie closed the distance between them gradually. She saw him sitting atop a large, overhanging boulder. Beanie had to use her hands in her scramble to climb it. At the top, Beanie turned around, worried about her mom. Way down the trail she saw her mother, climbing steadily but very slowly, making sure her feet were well placed before putting her weight on them. One cautious step at a time.

"Here she comes," Beanie said.

"Hooray! Finally!" Jerm shouted. Then he jumped up and scampered on again.

"Slow down, Jerm!" Mrs. Kingsley called in an irritated voice.

Beanie waited while her mother reached the boulder and leaned against it for support. Only then did Beanie take a long, deep breath and look around with satisfaction. The sky was a brilliant, clear blue like a blue china bowl. The breeze was cool and fresh.

"Isn't this a beautiful spot?" her mom asked.

"Yeah!" Beanie answered. "It's great."

They climbed slowly on for a half hour, crossing a shallow stream that trickled over mossy rocks. Beanie leaped over it. Jerm still ran ahead, singing either his Tumbledumble song or the Gingerbread Man rhyme, and calling out when he located the blue trail markers, which sometimes were high on trees, or faded and almost impossible to see. Beanie had to admit to herself that Jerm was actually very good at finding them. She wasn't sure she could have found all of them on her own.

Now Beanie clambered up a steep slope, badly eroded and laced with exposed tree roots. There was Jerm, sitting on a large rock. Behind him, the trail forked to both right and left.

"No more markers," Jerm announced glumly. "We're stuck."

"Sure there are," Beanie answered, glad for a chance to stop. "I'll find them. Give me a minute."

She looked around, scanning the tree trunks. She couldn't see any blue blazes either.

"Told ya," Jerm said. "I don't know which way we should go."

"I guess we'll have to wait," she said, and sat down next to Jerm.

After five minutes, Jerm asked, "Where's Mom?"

"I don't know. I thought she was right behind me."

"Hello down there!" Jerm yelled, his voice echoing through the trees. "Hey, Mom. Yoo-hoo!"

Beanie and Jerm listened intently, but the only sound they heard was the breeze rustling the leaves and an occasional birdcall. No one called back to them. Overhead, a branch popped loudly, and a chattering squirrel leaped for another tree. As he did, a cluster of acorns rattled to the ground.

"Whoa. It's kind of spooky up here," Jerm said. "Do you think we're lost?"

Beanie thought for a moment. "No. Maybe Mom had to go really, really slow. The trail's pretty steep. It's good you stopped here at this fork, Jerm, or we could have gotten majorly separated."

"Yeah. At least we have our whistles."

"What good's a whistle if there's no one there to hear it?"

"There's people here. There's other hikers," Jerm said in a small voice. "Remember those cars in the parking lot?"

"I guess so."

Although she'd gotten hot from climbing, now

Beanie was glad she was wearing jeans instead of shorts. The sweat on the surface of her skin had cooled quickly in the autumn breeze, and she shivered.

"Hey! I see someone," Jerm said. "Yo! Up here!"

In a few moments, two men hiked into view, each carrying a daypack, and both wearing baseball caps.

"They're Yankee fans," Jerm announced in a loud whisper. "Booo!"

"Jerm, be quiet. Hey there," Beanie said to the men. "Did you happen to pass a woman sitting by the side of the path?"

The men stopped at the large rock. "Yeah. She said she's all right, but I took her pulse," said the older of the two men. "It was pretty fast. And she said she'd been resting a few minutes."

"We offered to walk her down to the parking lot, but she thought she'd be able to get back on her own," the younger man said.

"Her doctor said it was okay for her to do normal activities," Beanie explained glumly.

"Boy, I don't know about that," the younger man said. "Maybe she ought to take a walk along the shore instead of climbing way the heck up here. That's your mom?"

"Yeah. I thought she was right behind us, but she wasn't," Beanie said.

"She's on the blue trail, maybe ten minutes back, near the stream. This path is pretty steep for the next mile at least. I think you ought to call it a day. Make sure you all stay together in the future, okay, young fella?" The older man looked right at Jerm.

"Yeah," he mumbled.

"We better get going. What do ya say, Bill?" the other man said.

"Guess we'll push off, then. Nice day," the older man said. "Enjoy it."

The men climbed the boulder and took the left-hand fork. "The trail's not so well marked on the way down. You two be careful. Stay together," the older man called out. They quickly disappeared from view.

"So? What are we going to do, Beanie?" Jerm asked.

"Turn back. We have to. We have to see how Mom's doing," Beanie said. "Come on."

"But I want to be the family champion hiker," Jerm said, jumping to his feet. "I want to go to the overlook like last year. It won't take long."

"No, Jerm. You can't. We have to find Mom."

"Oh, all right." He took off down the trail.

"Darn it! Get back here, Jeremiah!" Beanie called out. "Let's stay together on the way down. Didn't you hear what those guys just said?"

But Jerm didn't answer.

"Jeremiah!" she shouted, this time in utter exasperation.

There was no answer.

Who cared about a stupid view—blue water and some more trees? What if her mother had fallen or fainted? She plunged down the trail after Jerm, thinking he'd wait for her at the stream crossing.

When she reached the stream ten minutes later, no one was there. She jumped across, making the distance easily, and stood still, listening. All she heard was the gurgling of water as the little brook splashed over the moss-covered rocks in the streambed.

It was so very quiet on the mountainside, except for the wind in the trees. She heard no cars, no trucks, no planes. Occasionally a crow cawed, but that was all. She panicked a little and wondered if she was lost. But no. There were the blue blazes on the tree ahead. She was on the right trail.

She took out her whistle and blew on it, giving a long high-pitched blast. Then she listened. But again she heard nothing except the stream noises.

Abruptly she sat down on a fallen tree trunk. Probably Jerm and her mom had started back to the car, thinking she'd catch up. Maybe Jerm had told her mother that Beanie was only a few steps behind.

Or maybe Jerm had gotten lost on the way down. Aaah! Beanie punched a tree trunk. She was so tired of managing everybody! And she wasn't doing a very good job of it, either. Now her knuckles hurt from punching the tree.

She stood still, rubbing the pain from her fist. Looking around at the tossing branches above her head, she felt small and very alone. It had been a silly idea to come up Tumbledown on this hiking trip.

They knew Mrs. Kingsley would probably get

tired. But Beanie and Jerm had been excited about the climb. They'd done it twice before, once when Jerm was only four, so they hadn't thought about how Mom would actually manage it. Instead, they were pretending that they could still do the things they used to.

Now the hike was ruined. The older man was right. They should have gone to a picnic table in the shorefront park and eaten their sandwiches. Beanie got to her feet and sighed. She closed her eyes. Sometimes she resented her mother because she was sick. Always, always, always sick. Always resting. And there was nothing anybody could do.

Beanie realized that was how her daydreams about a new mother and a limousine had started. That was why she had offended her teacher and insulted Charles, her only real friend—because she was so angry that she wanted to run away. But she couldn't run away. She felt stuck on a merry-go-round of feelings. When she stopped feeling angry, then she felt helpless because her mom looked worn out. After that, Beanie felt guilty. As if maybe she should have helped out with chores more—cooking dinner, picking up around the house, entertaining Jerm. Dusting, doing laundry, even keeping track of overdue library books.

And after guilt came worry. For example, after seeing the few yellow leaves on the maples, she was worried about wintertime. The worst thing would be snow shoveling. Without her mom to help, how would she ever be able to clear the driveway by herself? Jerm was too young to lift a shovelful of heavy snow, especially the big chunks that the snowplow left behind at the end of the driveway. She would tell Uncle Ozzy about it. Maybe they could get a little snowblower, a shovel-sized one.

Beanie shifted her pack on her shoulders and started down the trail. Never mind the snow. There was nothing to do but take the next small step down the path. And then the next. Not looking too far ahead.

It was easy, really. But Beanie suddenly found herself pushing small, whiplike branches aside as she walked. She stopped and looked around. No blue blazes marked the trees. Anywhere.

Oh, no! She was off the trail. She backtracked until she reached the main trail, which turned out to be only a hundred yards away. There were the painted blue blazes again, each one just the size of a paintbrush. By now, surely she should have reached Jerm and her mother. She took out her whistle and blew on it as loudly as she could.

"Beanie," she heard faintly but clearly. "We're down here. In the parking lot."

⁓

"Well," her mother said as they lay on their sleeping bags in the tent to try them out and make sure they weren't lying on tree roots or hidden rocks. "So much for hiking."

"Yeah. We really, really stink at hiking," Jerm said. "But resting is going okay."

"Yeah. Lying down. We're good at that," Mrs. Kingsley said.

"Ahhh. This is the life," said Jerm, stretching out full length and wiggling his toes. His sneakers sat on the sand in front of the tent entrance.

"Mom, why did you even have us try to climb Tumbledown?" Beanie asked. "You could have fallen and gotten hurt or something. Jerm could have gotten lost."

Her mother didn't answer right away.

"Mom?"

"Because I want you guys to be able to do as many normal things as possible. And sometimes I don't know if I can do things or not until I try them. I guess I figure it's better to make the effort even if I screw up than it is to sit home all the time like a couch potato."

"But this was a bad idea. Mom, please, we need help. I think Mrs. Sprague might know some college students who are looking for a job. You could hire one to live at our house and do some chores. Maybe cook dinner once in a while. And shovel in the wintertime."

Her mother sighed. "Yeah. I've thought about having someone move in. But, Beanie, you and Jerm would have to share a bedroom."

Beanie hadn't thought about that for some reason. She and Jerm looked at each other for a long moment. Don't you dare screw this up now, Beanie thought, trying to send a mental message to her little brother.

"That's okay," Beanie said, swallowing hard. "I don't mind. I bet Jerm doesn't, either."

"Yeah. It might be fun," Jerm said. "I could even charge Beanie rent."

Mrs. Kingsley smiled and ruffled his hair.

"Mom. Cut that out!" he protested.

"Mom," said Beanie, "promise me when Uncle Ozzy comes you'll tell him everything we need. Okay?"

"Yes. Sorry I'm so stubborn, guys."

"I'm stubborn, too," Jerm announced.

"I'll say," Beanie said. "Why did you keep taking off on the trail?"

"I wanted to get to the overlook."

"You're a colossal pain." Now Beanie ruffled his hair.

"Hey! My do!" Jerm protested. "Hands off!"

Beanie crawled quickly out of the tent. "Can't catch me, Gingerbread Dude."

"Oh, yeah?" Jerm scrambled to his feet. "You're toast."

"No. You are!"

Beanie lunged away as he tried to swipe at her shirt. She ran around the picnic table with Jerm chasing her, then doubled back, caught him, and tackled him. In the tent, their mother dozed, obviously worn out.

15

THAT NIGHT, THEY DRAGGED SOME STICKS AND branches down to the shore. They made a circle of big rocks and lit a campfire at the edge of the lake. Then they lay on their backs on a quilt and watched the stars come out.

"You think we'll hear a loon now?" Jerm asked for the fiftieth time.

"I think that very bright star is Venus. Not a star but a planet," Mrs. Kingsley said.

"That's our next-door-neighbor planet," Jerm said.

"Right."

Beanie listened to their quiet voices and felt completely happy for the first time in months. Out here, with the stars overhead and the glow of a campfire, there seemed absolutely no point in worrying about anything, and she felt free, light, as if she had been lifted by a rising hot-air balloon.

In the middle of the night, Beanie woke up. She was wearing her soft fleece ski hat with the orange tassels, but the tip of her nose was icy cold where it poked out of the sleeping bag. She rose onto one elbow. Jerm was snoring softly, but her mother wasn't there. Even her sleeping bag was gone!

Beanie sat bolt upright, quietly unzipped the long sleeping-bag zipper, and crawled out of the front of the tent on her hands and knees, pushing her sneakers ahead of her. She pulled on her jacket.

The night was frosty and clear. Above her, the stars shone more brightly than before, looking closer to Earth and much clearer, bluer. She put on her sneakers and stood up, then looked around.

Where had her mother gone? Down to the night-black water?

Beanie thought she heard a sound. She took a few quiet steps forward and listened again. The sound was more noticeable now. Was that huddled shape down at the edge of the lake her mother, crying?

Beanie approached the water. "Mom?"

The huddled form moved. Her mom, wrapped in her sleeping bag, turned her head. "Hi, Beanie. Come on down here."

Beanie ran across the narrow margin of sand that skirted the lake shore. Her mom was using the sleeping bag as a blanket. Beanie climbed in between her mother's knees and leaned her head back on her mother's chest. Her mom hugged her and sighed.

"Why are you crying?" Beanie asked.

"Oh, because of today. I feel like I've let you guys down so badly."

"Because of the CFS, you mean?"

"Yeah. Not being able to do the hike today made me realize that we have to reconsider absolutely everything—from making dinner to going for walks. I'm just not going to be the kind of mom I thought I would be for you."

"What? How can you say that?" Beanie said. "You're perfect. You haven't changed. You're exactly the same as before. I mean . . ." She thought for a minute. "I mean you're still you. You're . . . well, you still know me. Even my secrets. You're the one and only Madame Squidley, right?"

Her mother laughed, then said in a heavy accent, "Yes. Of course. Give me your hand, my dear. The great Squidley cannot be refused."

Beanie stuck out her hand, and her mother shone a flashlight on it. "You know everything, Squidley. Like which star is which. And what happened to me at the festival. And you brought me an apple when I was a jerk at school."

"No, I do not know everything. I didn't know how badly I'd do hiking!"

Beanie thought for a moment. "But you knew you had to find out."

"Ah, you brilliant child. Now, let me consult the powers of the universe. Where is your line of destiny? Yes, here it is. This big, long one. But, wait, what's this? Crisscrossing lines? Confusion? That must represent us out here in the woods, blundering around." Her mother laughed again. "We must have been quite a sight—Jerm racing off one way, you stressed out in the middle, and me sitting on the ground like a lump! Some hike."

But Beanie was thinking about how a few minutes ago she had truly thought that her mother was perfect. Now she knew that Mrs. Adams, the secret mother she had daydreamed about for weeks and weeks, wouldn't do for her and Jerm at all. Mrs. Adams might have a tennis trophy in the living room, but she had never once come out to play four square in the road. She would never even think about going hiking. And Beanie was sure she couldn't possibly be Madame Squidley. Beanie loved her mother fiercely.

"But, Mom? Are you absolutely sure you won't get worse?" she asked in a tiny voice. The tears in her eyes made the stars sparkle even more brightly.

"Ninety percent sure, okay? And, yes, your palm says you will have a long and happy life with lots of great and wonderful crisscrossing things happening to you. Don't worry about me, Beanie. I might even have better days. It's possible. Maybe in five years there will be medicine or something. Who knows? We just can't tell."

Beanie snuggled closer to her mom, who hugged her tightly. "But in the meantime, there's no one to take care of you," Beanie whispered.

"No. There isn't. We just have to be matter-of-fact about that. No self-pity allowed. That's the rule I have for myself, remember? Now we have to get back in the sleeping bags so we don't get completely chilled."

"But, Mom? There's another thing. I haven't been nice to Charles."

"Oh, Beanie." She heard the disappointment in her mother's voice. "Charles is a good friend."

"I know."

"Yeah? Come on, Beanie. Let's go."

———

"I hear one! I hear one. Mom! Beanie! Wake up!"

Jerm poked her, then shook her. "Ugh. Jerm! Cut it out!" Beanie groaned, checking her watch. "Leave me alone. It's six o'clock in the morning."

"Shhh," he said. "Listen."

They heard a long, spooky hooting—the cry of a loon. Then one answering call.

"There!" Jerm said. "That makes this a perfect trip."

———

On Sunday afternoon, as soon as they got home and unpacked the car, which Beanie and Jerm had to do by themselves in small steps while their mom rested, Beanie hurried across the street, eager now to finally apologize to Charles. His dad's car was parked in the driveway, so she knew Charles was back. His parents must be inside, having the big discussion Charles had told her about.

As Beanie rang the front doorbell, she could hear

loud, angry voices. "You forbade him to wear it all weekend?" she heard his mother ask angrily. "I can't believe you."

"You know he's getting a real complex about this? All because of that brace. Just let him grow out of the scoliosis on his own. He should be out playing sports with the other guys."

"He won't grow out of it," Charles's mother argued. "That's the point. His muscles need to grow straight and strengthen now so that his back and shoulders don't sag as he gets taller."

"That thing he wears makes him look handicapped. He's not wearing it in my house," his father shouted.

If Charles was upstairs, he must have heard every word of what his father was saying. Beanie rang the bell again. No one came to answer the door. Beanie knew she shouldn't listen in, but she couldn't tear herself away.

"You don't leave us any choice, then. Either he wears it on weekends at your house, or he's going to have to start wearing it to school," Charles's mother said.

But he doesn't want to wear it to school, Beanie wanted to shout. She rang the doorbell again, twice. Now she heard approaching footsteps.

Mrs. Sprague opened the door. "Yes, Beanie?"

"Is Charles home?"

"Uhh, no. He's not in the house. He's outside somewhere," she said, and shut the door quickly.

Beanie peeked into the two cars parked in the driveway. Not there. She walked around the whole yard. No Charles. She ran home and checked the hammock. No Charles. She stood in the middle of the street and yelled at the top of her lungs, "Charles!"

No answer.

She stood still in the middle of the road. She was sure he was hiding. He hated it when his parents argued, especially when they argued about him. She knew he'd feel terrible if he had to wear that big brace all day in school. Boys would pick on him, and he had no buddies to back him up. He'd never get on teams at recess or in gym.

Where would Charles go if she, his best friend, weren't home, and he was feeling terrible? "I know. The frog pond," Beanie said out loud.

16

"CHARLES! HEY, CHARLES!" BEANIE CALLED AS she approached the frog pond.

She saw something big, white, and plastic sitting in the shallow, muddy water. It was Charles's back brace. Charles poked his head out of their old tree branch shelter. She could tell he'd been crying.

"Hi," she said, stopping cautiously ten feet away.

"What do you want?"

"Did you throw your brace in the pond?"

"Yeah."

"Move over. I'm coming in."

Beanie got down on her hands and knees and crawled into the shelter with Charles. "I went over to your house," she said.

Charles grunted in reply.

"I could hear your parents arguing when I rang the doorbell."

"I hate them. Both of them. They always fight about my scoliosis. I hate that."

"Maybe they like arguing," Beanie said. "Maybe they'd argue anyway, even if you didn't have scoliosis."

He laughed a little.

"Yeah, maybe. Here." He reached into his pocket and pulled out a small scrap of paper with several names and phone numbers on it. "These are the names of some students who are looking for housing."

"Wow! Thanks. I already persuaded my mom to get a student to live with us. So I know she'll call. But, Charles, about you, wouldn't it help if you wore your brace to school and everywhere?"

"Probably. Yeah," said Charles.

"So why don't you stop trying to hide it? Why don't you start wearing it to school? Then your dad will have to shut up because you'll be the boss of when you wear it. Besides, I think you should wear it more if it might help your back so you'll be okay in high school."

"Yeah."

They sat quietly, thinking about this.

"The kids will tease me. I hardly have any friends as it is," Charles said.

"Yeah, but I don't have friends either. So? We'll just stand up for ourselves. We have more fun than they do. Whatever we do, we can't feel sorry for ourselves."

"Yeah, I guess."

Beanie got to her feet, pulled off her sneakers and socks, and rolled up the bottoms of her jeans. She crawled out of the hideout, over dead branches and twigs, picking her way to the edge of the pond. She stepped in.

"Ooh! Eeeh! Aaah!" The mud was startlingly cold.

Gingerly she stepped deeper into the muddy water. The silky-soft mud clouded up and squished between her toes. She turned and made a face. "Ugh. This feels awful!"

She waded out farther, pulling her jeans higher to keep them out of the brown water. Then she leaned way forward and grabbed the cushiony edge of the brace. She picked it up and carried it dripping from the pond.

"Here you go." She handed it to Charles.

"Thanks, Beanie," he said.

"I'm sorry I was so mean to you before," she said. "I've been kind of worried and stressed out, ever since we went to the Lobster Festival."

"I know. That's okay."

"So. There it is. Go ahead. Put it on."

"Now? When it's soaking wet?"

"Sure. Smelly. Muddy. Put that sucker on."

Laughing, Charles crawled out of the hut and strapped the brace into place around his waist, then did a silly hula dance. "How do I look?"

"Awesome. Your dad will flip when you show up like this!" Beanie said, laughing. "I wish I had one, too. We could really freak him out."

They walked back home. Charles's father's car was still parked in their driveway.

"See ya. Oh, by the way," Beanie added, "I'm making you a present. Actually, Madame Squidley is helping me. You're going to love it." Then Beanie headed for the back door.

She spent a large part of Sunday evening getting Charles's lawn chair ready. They had to make an emergency trip to Wal-Mart to look for Christmas lights. They couldn't find any, so Beanie bought a string of little orange pumpkin lights for his chair instead.

She carried the four chairs upstairs and set them up in the living room. Jerm brought the surge protector from the computer plug so all the lights could be plugged in at once. They sat in the chairs.

Then Jerm bolted from the room. He returned in his slug-hunting outfit: Red Sox baseball cap, life jacket, hideous tropical-print shorts, long underwear, a red clip-on bow tie, and a fake nose/eyeglass mask.

"Going on a slug hunt, going on a slug hunt, I'm not afraid, I'm not afraid," he sang. "Hey, can we go out and look for slugs right now, Mom?"

"Oh, Jerm, not now. I'm trying to think. Let's see." In her bedroom, Mrs. Kingsley was laying out her clothes for the coming week.

"You know, it's funny, but I can't remember what clothes I have, let alone what day it is," she said. "So I thought I'd line them all up at once for the whole week and just work my way down the pile as the days go by."

"Mom?" Jerm repeated. "About the slugs. Can we go hunting now? I mean all of us."

But Mrs. Kingsley didn't answer. "I thought I had a plaid skirt. And I know I had some low-heeled black pumps. I think. Or maybe that was a few years back."

"You don't have any black pumps, Mom," Beanie said.

"No? Really?" Her mother came into the living room and sat down on the sofa. "I feel so confused. I never feel sure of anything, especially about when things happened or how to get places. I can't even remember the roads to take when I get downtown. I can't picture them in my mind."

"Mom!" roared Jerm. "I said can we go out and—"

"Jerm! Stop!"

He burst into tears. Mrs. Kingsley dropped the skirt she was holding and hugged him.

"I'm sorry, Jerm. I just made a big mistake. I should never have yelled at you like that."

"You scared me, Mom," Jerm said, sobbing.

"Me too," Beanie said in a shaky voice.

Mrs. Kingsley said, "I get confused. Loud noises make it much worse. There are just so many things to remember at once. And I simply can't remember. It's like being lost."

"Is it foggy?" Beanie asked. "Is it a sorrowful fog?"

"Very sorrowful. As though the glue of life had vanished and everything was floating around just out of reach. Just when you think you've got it, there's nothing there to hold on to. It's very weird."

"Mom," said Beanie. "It's time. Now."

"Yes, I know. As soon as I finish this, I'll start calling those students and set up some interviews."

"And then," said Jerm, sniffling, "can we go out and look for slugs?"

"How about tomorrow? I'm so worn out from the trip that I wouldn't enjoy hunting slugs today. We'll look for slugs tomorrow night. Okay? And if I forget, I'm sure you'll remind me."

Jerm nodded. "I won't forget."

Beanie went to the kitchen phone and called Charles. "Hey. Guess what? I finished your present. Come over tomorrow night and we can use it."

"Oh? Use it? At night? Is it some kind of flashlight?"

"Nope."

"A telescope?"

"Nope."

"Come on. You can tell me."

"Nope," said Beanie.

"Guess what. I told my parents that I was in charge of my brace from now on. And I told them I would call my doctor and discuss it with him, just like you did with Dr. Howell. Tomorrow I'm wearing my car seat to school," Charles said.

"You called it a car seat," Beanie pointed out.

"Yeah, I know. That's because it looks like one. And also, I figured it would be a good way to show the kids I can handle a little teasing. So this way, it will seem like I gave it a name first. Pretty clever, huh?"

"Yeah. I'm impressed!" Beanie said. "See ya." She hung up and called out to her mother, "Mom! Your turn!"

17

When Charles got on the bus the next morning, he was wearing his back brace.

"Sit by me!" Beanie called out as soon as she saw him.

Charles slid into the seat beside her.

"We have band today," Beanie said.

"Yeah, I brought my sticks." He pointed to a side pocket in his backpack. The tops of his new drumsticks poked out.

Miranda edged her way up the aisle, pausing at their seat. "Whoa, Charles. You're wearing your brace thing to school?" she asked incredulously.

"Yeah."

"Oh, my God. Kids are going to make so much fun of you," she said, hurrying past.

"I'm not," Beanie said loudly. "And I'm a kid."

Charles whispered, "There. See what I mean about her? She's a complete snob."

"But her mom is nice," Beanie said, reluctant to part with her image of Mrs. Adams. "I think."

"I bet secretly her mom is a snob, too. Otherwise, how would Miranda have gotten so good at it?"

"Maybe."

When they got off the bus, Charles and Beanie decided to skip morning playground and went straight to Miss Bennett's room. She was writing a cursive lesson on the board.

"Hi, Miss Bennett," Charles said.

"We want to talk to you about something," Beanie said.

"I'm going to be wearing my brace to school from now on."

"Yeah. And I came to tell you my mom has been really sick and it makes me feel worried," Beanie said, to her own surprise. "The doctor can't help her."

Miss Bennett stared at them.

"So when the kids come inside today, I want to explain to the class about my brace," Charles said.

"Yeah, and we don't care if we never have any friends in our whole lives," Beanie added.

"Well, I . . . Umm, sure. I mean, of course you can talk to the class, Charles," Miss Bennett said, stumbling over her words.

"Good. Now can we have a library pass? We'll wait there for the bell," Charles said. "I don't want to have to go out on the playground before I talk to the kids."

Without a word, Miss Bennett handed them the piece of wood that said LIBRARY/ROOM 14 on it. They hurried down the hall.

As they rounded the corner of the fifth-grade wing, they nearly smacked into— Was it Ernestine barreling along with her trumpet case? She had a shag haircut and was wearing a short pretend-leather jacket instead of her usual mohair sweater.

"Hey! Hi, Ernestine," Beanie said.

But Ernestine brushed by them without answering.

"Ooh. She's not talking to us. Can you believe it? A brand-new member of the Snob Squad, I guess," Beanie said.

"Who cares?" Charles said.

"Hey, Charles! You were awesome with Miss Bennett," Beanie said.

"Thanks. You know, maybe we've been handling grownups wrong all along. We should do what you did when you called your mom's doctor. You just went at him head on."

"Yeah," Beanie acknowledged. "I did."

"So that's what I did to Miss Bennett. I don't think she knows how to deal with us."

"Yeah."

"I'm going to do the same thing with the kids," Charles said. "Tackle 'em head on."

"Go for it, dude," Beanie answered.

"I will. You'll see."

Beanie and Charles grinned at each other, leaned back in the library chairs with their arms folded, and waited for the morning bell.